Notes to The Complete Poetical Works of Percy Bysshe Shelley

Mary W. Shelley

Contents

PREFACE BY MRS. SHELLEY TO FIRST COLLECTED EDITION, 1839. 7

POSTSCRIPT IN SECOND EDITION OF 1839. 12

PREFACE BY MRS. SHELLEY 13

NOTE ON QUEEN MAB, BY MRS. SHELLEY...17

NOTE ON "ALASTOR", BY MRS. SHELLEY. 24

NOTE ON THE "REVOLT OF ISLAM", BY MRS. SHELLEY. 26

NOTE ON ROSALIND AND HELEN BY MRS. SHELLEY...30

NOTE ON "PROMETHEUS UNBOUND", BY MRS. SHELLEY. 32

NOTE ON THE CENCI, BY MRS. SHELLEY. 40

NOTE ON THE MASK OF ANARCHY, BY MRS. SHELLEY. 46

NOTE ON PETER BELL THE THIRD, BY MRS. SHELLEY..48

NOTE ON THE WITCH OF ATLAS, BY MRS. SHELLEY. 49

NOTE ON OEDIPUS TYRANNUS, BY MRS. SHELLEY..51

NOTE ON HELLAS, BY MRS. SHELLEY. 53

NOTE ON THE EARLY POEMS, BY MRS. SHELLEY. 56

NOTE ON POEMS OF 1816, BY MRS. SHELLEY..58

NOTE ON POEMS OF 1817, BY MRS. SHELLEY..59

NOTE ON POEMS OF 1818, BY MRS. SHELLEY..61

NOTE ON POEMS OF 1819, BY MRS. SHELLEY..63

NOTE ON POEMS OF 1820, BY MRS. SHELLEY..64

NOTE ON POEMS OF 1821, BY MRS. SHELLEY..66

NOTE ON POEMS OF 1822, BY MRS. SHELLEY..70

NOTES TO THE COMPLETE POETICAL WORKS OF

PERCY BYSSHE SHELLEY

BY

Mary W. Shelley

PREFACE BY MRS. SHELLEY

TO FIRST COLLECTED EDITION, 1839.

Obstacles have long existed to my presenting the public with a perfect
edition of Shelley's Poems. These being at last happily removed, I
hasten to fulfil an important duty,--that of giving the productions of a
sublime genius to the world, with all the correctness possible, and of,
at the same time, detailing the history of those productions, as they
sprang, living and warm, from his heart and brain. I abstain from any
remark on the occurrences of his private life, except inasmuch as the
passions which they engendered inspired his poetry. This is not the time
to relate the truth; and I should reject any colouring of the truth. No
account of these events has ever been given at all approaching reality
in their details, either as regards himself or others; nor shall I
further allude to them than to remark that the errors of action
committed by a man as noble and generous as Shelley, may, as far as he
only is concerned, be fearlessly avowed by those who loved him, in the
firm conviction that, were they judged impartially, his character would
stand in fairer and brighter light than that of any contemporary.
Whatever faults he had ought to find extenuation among his fellows,
since they prove him to be human; without them, the exalted nature of
his soul would have raised him into something divine.

The qualities that struck any one newly introduced to Shelley
were,--First, a gentle and cordial goodness that animated his

intercourse with warm affection and helpful sympathy. The other, the eagerness and ardour with which he was attached to the cause of human happiness and improvement; and the fervent eloquence with which he discussed such subjects. His conversation was marked by its happy abundance, and the beautiful language in which he clothed his poetic ideas and philosophical notions. To defecate life of its misery and its evil was the ruling passion of his soul; he dedicated to it every power of his mind, every pulsation of his heart. He looked on political freedom as the direct agent to effect the happiness of mankind; and thus any new-sprung hope of liberty inspired a joy and an exultation more intense and wild than he could have felt for any personal advantage. Those who have never experienced the workings of passion on general and unselfish subjects cannot understand this; and it must be difficult of comprehension to the younger generation rising around, since they cannot remember the scorn and hatred with which the partisans of reform were regarded some few years ago, nor the persecutions to which they were exposed. He had been from youth the victim of the state of feeling inspired by the reaction of the French Revolution; and believing firmly in the justice and excellence of his views, it cannot be wondered that a nature as sensitive, as impetuous, and as generous as his, should put its whole force into the attempt to alleviate for others the evils of those systems from which he had himself suffered. Many advantages attended his birth; he spurned them all when balanced with what he considered his duties. He was generous to imprudence, devoted to heroism.

These characteristics breathe throughout his poetry. The struggle for human weal; the resolution firm to martyrdom; the impetuous pursuit, the glad triumph in good; the determination not to despair; --such were the features that marked those of his works which he regarded with most complacency, as sustained by a lofty subject and useful aim.

In addition to these, his poems may be divided into two classes,--the purely imaginative, and those which sprang from the emotions of his heart. Among the former may be classed the "Witch of Atlas", "Adonais", and his latest composition, left imperfect, the "Triumph of Life". In the first of these particularly he gave the reins to his fancy, and luxuriated in every idea as it rose; in all there is that sense of mystery which formed an essential portion of his perception of life--a clinging to the subtler inner spirit, rather than to the outward form--a curious and metaphysical anatomy of human passion and perception.

The second class is, of course, the more popular, as appealing at once to emotions common to us all; some of these rest on the passion of love; others on grief and despondency; others on the sentiments inspired by natural objects. Shelley's conception of love was exalted, absorbing, allied to all that is purest and noblest in our nature, and warmed by earnest passion; such it appears when he gave it a voice in verse. Yet he was usually averse to expressing these feelings, except when highly idealized; and many of his more beautiful effusions he had cast aside unfinished, and they were never seen by me till after I had lost him. Others, as for instance "Rosalind and Helen" and "Lines written among the Euganean Hills", I found among his papers by chance; and with some difficulty urged him to complete them. There are others, such as the "Ode to the Skylark and The Cloud", which, in the opinion of many critics, bear a purer poetical stamp than any other of his productions. They were written as his mind prompted: listening to the carolling of the bird, aloft in the azure sky of Italy; or marking the cloud as it sped across the heavens, while he floated in his boat on the Thames.

No poet was ever warmed by a more genuine and unforced inspiration. His extreme sensibility gave the intensity of passion to his intellectual pursuits; and rendered his mind keenly alive to every perception of outward objects, as well as to his internal sensations. Such a gift is, among the sad vicissitudes of human life, the disappointments we meet, and the galling sense of our own mistakes and errors, fraught with pain;

to escape from such, he delivered up his soul to poetry, and felt happy when he sheltered himself, from the influence of human sympathies, in the wildest regions of fancy. His imagination has been termed too brilliant, his thoughts too subtle. He loved to idealize reality; and this is a taste shared by few. We are willing to have our passing whims exalted into passions, for this gratifies our vanity; but few of us understand or sympathize with the endeavour to ally the love of abstract beauty, and adoration of abstract good, the to agathon kai to kalon of the Socratic philosophers, with our sympathies with our kind. In this, Shelley resembled Plato; both taking more delight in the abstract and the ideal than in the special and tangible. This did not result from imitation; for it was not till Shelley resided in Italy that he made Plato his study. He then translated his "Symposium" and his "Ion"; and the English language boasts of no more brilliant composition than Plato's Praise of Love translated by Shelley. To return to his own poetry. The luxury of imagination, which sought nothing beyond itself (as a child burdens itself with spring flowers, thinking of no use beyond the enjoyment of gathering them), often showed itself in his verses: they will be only appreciated by minds which have resemblance to his own; and the mystic subtlety of many of his thoughts will share the same fate. The metaphysical strain that characterizes much of what he has written was, indeed, the portion of his works to which, apart from those whose scope was to awaken mankind to aspirations for what he considered the true and good, he was himself particularly attached. There is much, however, that speaks to the many. When he would consent to dismiss these huntings after the obscure (which, entwined with his nature as they were, he did with difficulty), no poet ever expressed in sweeter, more heart-reaching, or more passionate verse, the gentler or more forcible emotions of the soul.

A wise friend once wrote to Shelley: 'You are still very young, and in certain essential respects you do not yet sufficiently perceive that you are so.' It is seldom that the young know what youth is, till they have got beyond its period; and time was not given him to attain this knowledge. It must be remembered that there is the stamp of such inexperience on all he wrote; he had not completed his nine-and-twentieth year when he died. The calm of middle life did not add the seal of the virtues which adorn maturity to those generated by the vehement spirit of youth. Through life also he was a martyr to ill-health, and constant pain wound up his nerves to a pitch of susceptibility that rendered his views of life different from those of a man in the enjoyment of healthy sensations. Perfectly gentle and forbearing in manner, he suffered a good deal of internal irritability, or rather excitement, and his fortitude to bear was almost always on the stretch; and thus, during a short life, he had gone through more experience of sensation than many whose existence is protracted. 'If I die to-morrow,' he said, on the eve of his unanticipated death, 'I have lived to be older than my father.' The weight of thought and feeling burdened him heavily; you read his sufferings in his attenuated frame, while you perceived the mastery he held over them in his animated countenance and brilliant eyes.

He died, and the world showed no outward sign. But his influence over mankind, though slow in growth, is fast augmenting; and, in the ameliorations that have taken place in the political state of his country, we may trace in part the operation of his arduous struggles. His spirit gathers peace in its new state from the sense that, though late, his exertions were not made in vain, and in the progress of the liberty he so fondly loved.

He died, and his place, among those who knew him intimately, has never been filled up. He walked beside them like a spirit of good to comfort and benefit--to enlighten the darkness of life with irradiations of genius, to cheer it with his sympathy and love. Any one, once attached to Shelley, must feel all other affections, however true and fond, as wasted on barren soil in comparison. It is our best consolation to know that such a pure-minded and exalted being was once among us, and now exists where we hope one day to join him; -- although the intolerant, in their blindness, poured down anathemas, the Spirit of Good, who can judge the heart, never rejected him.

In the notes appended to the poems I have endeavoured to narrate the origin and history of each. The loss of nearly all letters and papers which refer to his early life renders the execution more imperfect than it would otherwise have been. I have, however, the liveliest recollection of all that was done and said during the period of my knowing him. Every impression is as clear as if stamped yesterday, and I have no apprehension of any mistake in my statements as far as they go. In other respects I am indeed incompetent: but I feel the importance of the task, and regard it as my most sacred duty. I endeavour to fulfil it in a manner he would himself approve; and hope, in this publication, to lay the first stone of a monument due to Shelley's genius, his sufferings, and his virtues:--

> Se al seguir son tarda,
> Forse avverra che 'l bel nome gentile
> Consacrero con questa stanca penna.

POSTSCRIPT IN SECOND EDITION OF 1839.

In revising this new edition, and carefully consulting Shelley's scattered and confused papers, I found a few fragments which had hitherto escaped me, and was enabled to complete a few poems hitherto left unfinished. What at one time escapes the searching eye, dimmed by its own earnestness, becomes clear at a future period. By the aid of a friend, I also present some poems complete and correct which hitherto have been defaced by various mistakes and omissions. It was suggested that the poem "To the Queen of my Heart" was falsely attributed to Shelley. I certainly find no trace of it among his papers; and, as those of his intimate friends whom I have consulted never heard of it, I omit it.

Two poems are added of some length, "Swellfoot the Tyrant" and "Peter Bell the Third". I have mentioned the circumstances under which they were written in the notes; and need only add that they are conceived in a very different spirit from Shelley's usual compositions. They are specimens of the burlesque and fanciful; but, although they adopt a familiar style and homely imagery, there shine through the radiance of the poet's imagination the earnest views and opinions of the politician and the moralist.

At my request the publisher has restored the omitted passages of "Queen Mab". I now present this edition as a complete collection of my husband's poetical works, and I do not foresee that I can hereafter add to or take away a word or line.

Putney, November 6, 1839.

PREFACE BY MRS. SHELLEY

TO THE VOLUME OF POSTHUMOUS POEMS PUBLISHED IN 1824.

> In nobil sangue vita umile e queta,
> Ed in alto intelletto un puro core
> Frutto senile in sul giovenil fibre,
> E in aspetto pensoso anima lieta.--PETRARCA.

It had been my wish, on presenting the public with the Posthumous Poems of Mr. Shelley, to have accompanied them by a biographical notice; as it appeared to me that at this moment a narration of the events of my husband's life would come more gracefully from other hands than mine, I applied to Mr. Leigh Hunt. The distinguished friendship that Mr. Shelley felt for him, and the enthusiastic affection with which Mr. Leigh Hunt clings to his friend's memory, seemed to point him out as the person best calculated for such an undertaking. His absence from this country, which prevented our mutual explanation, has unfortunately rendered my scheme abortive. I do not doubt but that on some other occasion he will pay this tribute to his lost friend, and sincerely regret that the volume which I edit has not been honoured by its insertion.

The comparative solitude in which Mr. Shelley lived was the occasion that he was personally known to few; and his fearless enthusiasm in the cause which he considered the most sacred upon earth, the improvement of the moral and physical state of mankind, was the chief reason why he, like other illustrious reformers, was pursued by hatred and calumny. No man was ever more devoted than he to the endeavour of making those around him happy; no man ever possessed friends more unfeignedly attached to him. The ungrateful world did not feel his loss, and the gap it made seemed to close as quickly over his memory as the murderous sea above his living frame. Hereafter men will lament that his transcendent powers of intellect were extinguished before they had bestowed on them their choicest treasures. To his friends his loss is irremediable: the wise, the brave, the gentle, is gone for ever! He is to them as a bright vision, whose radiant track, left behind in the memory, is worth all the realities that society can afford. Before the critics contradict me, let them appeal to any one who had ever known him. To see him was to love him: and his presence, like Ithuriel's spear, was alone sufficient to disclose the falsehood of the tale which his enemies whispered in the ear of the ignorant world.

His life was spent in the contemplation of Nature, in arduous study, or in acts of kindness and affection. He was an elegant scholar and a profound metaphysician; without possessing much scientific knowledge, he was unrivalled in the justness and extent of his observations on natural objects; he knew every plant by its name, and was familiar with the history and habits of every production of the earth; he could interpret without a fault each appearance in the sky; and the varied phenomena of heaven and earth filled him with deep emotion. He made his study and reading-room of the shadowed copse, the stream, the lake, and the waterfall. Ill health and continual pain preyed upon his powers; and the solitude in which we lived, particularly on our first arrival in Italy, although congenial to his feelings, must frequently have weighed upon his spirits; those beautiful and affecting "Lines written in Dejection near Naples" were composed at such an interval; but, when in health, his spirits were buoyant and youthful to an extraordinary degree.

Such was his love for Nature that every page of his poetry is associated, in the minds of his friends, with the loveliest scenes of the countries which he inhabited. In early life he visited the most beautiful parts of this country and Ireland. Afterwards the Alps of Switzerland became his inspirers. "Prometheus Unbound" was written among the deserted and flower-grown ruins of Rome; and, when he made his home under the Pisan hills, their roofless recesses harboured him as he composed the "Witch of Atlas", "Adonais", and "Hellas". In the wild but beautiful Bay of Spezzia, the winds and waves which he loved became his playmates. His days were chiefly spent on the water; the management of his boat, its alterations and improvements, were his principal occupation. At night, when the unclouded moon shone on the calm sea, he often went alone in his little shallop to the rocky caves that bordered it, and, sitting beneath their shelter, wrote the "Triumph of Life", the last of his productions. The beauty but strangeness of this lonely place, the refined pleasure which he felt in the companionship of a few selected friends, our entire sequestration from the rest of the world, all contributed to render this period of his life one of continued enjoyment. I am convinced that the two months we passed there were the happiest which he had ever known: his health even rapidly improved, and he was never better than when I last saw him, full of spirits and joy, embark for Leghorn, that he might there welcome Leigh Hunt to Italy. I was to have accompanied him; but illness confined me to my room, and thus put the seal on my misfortune. His vessel bore out of sight with a favourable wind, and I remained awaiting his return by the breakers of that sea which was about to engulf him.

He spent a week at Pisa, employed in kind offices toward his friend, and enjoying with keen delight the renewal of their intercourse. He then embarked with Mr. Williams, the chosen and beloved sharer of his pleasures and of his fate, to return to us. We waited for them in vain; the sea by its restless moaning seemed to desire to inform us of what we would not learn:--but a veil may well be drawn over such misery. The real anguish of those moments transcended all the fictions that the most glowing imagination ever portrayed; our seclusion, the savage nature of the inhabitants of the surrounding villages, and our immediate vicinity to the troubled sea, combined to imbue with strange horror our days of uncertainty. The truth was at last known,--a truth that made our loved and lovely Italy appear a tomb, its sky a pall. Every heart echoed the deep lament, and my only consolation was in the praise and earnest love that each voice bestowed and each countenance demonstrated for him we had lost,--not, I fondly hope, for ever; his unearthly and elevated nature is a pledge of the continuation of his being, although in an altered form. Rome received his ashes; they are deposited beneath its weed-grown wall, and 'the world's sole monument' is enriched by his remains.

I must add a few words concerning the contents of this volume. "Julian and Maddalo", the "Witch of Atlas", and most of the "Translations", were written some years ago; and, with the exception of the "Cyclops", and the Scenes from the "Magico Prodigioso", may be considered as having received the author's ultimate corrections. The "Triumph of Life" was his last work, and was left in so unfinished a state that I arranged it in its present form with great difficulty. All his poems which were scattered in periodical works are collected in this volume, and I have

added a reprint of "Alastor, or the Spirit of Solitude": the difficulty
with which a copy can be obtained is the cause of its republication.
Many of the Miscellaneous Poems, written on the spur of the occasion,
and never retouched, I found among his manuscript books, and have
carefully copied. I have subjoined, whenever I have been able, the date
of their composition.

I do not know whether the critics will reprehend the insertion of some
of the most imperfect among them; but I frankly own that I have been
more actuated by the fear lest any monument of his genius should escape
me than the wish of presenting nothing but what was complete to the
fastidious reader. I feel secure that the lovers of Shelley's poetry
(who know how, more than any poet of the present day, every line and
word he wrote is instinct with peculiar beauty) will pardon and thank
me: I consecrate this volume to them.

The size of this collection has prevented the insertion of any prose
pieces. They will hereafter appear in a separate publication.

MARY W. SHELLEY.

London, June 1, 1824.

NOTE ON QUEEN MAB, BY MRS. SHELLEY.

Shelley was eighteen when he wrote "Queen Mab"; he never published it.
When it was written, he had come to the decision that he was too young
to be a 'judge of controversies'; and he was desirous of acquiring 'that
sobriety of spirit which is the characteristic of true heroism.' But he
never doubted the truth or utility of his opinions; and, in printing and
privately distributing "Queen Mab", he believed that he should further
their dissemination, without occasioning the mischief either to others
or himself that might arise from publication. It is doubtful whether he

would himself have admitted it into a collection of his works. His severe classical taste, refined by the constant study of the Greek poets, might have discovered defects that escape the ordinary reader; and the change his opinions underwent in many points would have prevented him from putting forth the speculations of his boyish days. But the poem is too beautiful in itself, and far too remarkable as the production of a boy of eighteen, to allow of its being passed over: besides that, having been frequently reprinted, the omission would be vain. In the former edition certain portions were left out, as shocking the general reader from the violence of their attack on religion. I myself had a painful feeling that such erasures might be looked upon as a mark of disrespect towards the author, and am glad to have the opportunity of restoring them. The notes also are reprinted entire--not because they are models of reasoning or lessons of truth, but because Shelley wrote them, and that all that a man at once so distinguished and so excellent ever did deserves to be preserved. The alterations his opinions underwent ought to be recorded, for they form his history.

A series of articles was published in the "New Monthly Magazine" during the autumn of the year 1832, written by a man of great talent, a fellow-collegian and warm friend of Shelley: they describe admirably the state of his mind during his collegiate life. Inspired with ardour for the acquisition of knowledge, endowed with the keenest sensibility and with the fortitude of a martyr, Shelley came among his fellow-creatures, congregated for the purposes of education, like a spirit from another sphere; too delicately organized for the rough treatment man uses towards man, especially in the season of youth, and too resolute in carrying out his own sense of good and justice, not to become a victim. To a devoted attachment to those he loved he added a determined resistance to oppression. Refusing to fag at Eton, he was treated with revolting cruelty by masters and boys: this roused instead of taming his spirit, and he rejected the duty of obedience when it was enforced by menaces and punishment. To aversion to the society of his fellow-creatures, such as he found them when collected together in societies, where one egged on the other to acts of tyranny, was joined the deepest sympathy and compassion; while the attachment he felt for individuals, and the admiration with which he regarded their powers and their virtues, led him to entertain a high opinion of the perfectibility of human nature; and he believed that all could reach the highest grade of moral improvement, did not the customs and prejudices of society foster evil passions and excuse evil actions.

The oppression which, trembling at every nerve yet resolute to heroism, it was his ill-fortune to encounter at school and at college, led him to dissent in all things from those whose arguments were blows, whose faith appeared to engender blame and hatred. 'During my existence,' he wrote to a friend in 1812, 'I have incessantly speculated, thought, and read.' His readings were not always well chosen; among them were the works of the French philosophers: as far as metaphysical argument went, he temporarily became a convert. At the same time, it was the cardinal article of his faith that, if men were but taught and induced to treat their fellows with love, charity, and equal rights, this earth would realize paradise. He looked upon religion, as it is professed, and above all practised, as hostile instead of friendly to the cultivation of those virtues which would make men brothers.

Can this be wondered at? At the age of seventeen, fragile in health and frame, of the purest habits in morals, full of devoted generosity and universal kindness, glowing with ardour to attain wisdom, resolved at every personal sacrifice to do right, burning with a desire for affection and sympathy,--he was treated as a reprobate, cast forth as a criminal.

The cause was that he was sincere; that he believed the opinions which he entertained to be true. And he loved truth with a martyr's love; he was ready to sacrifice station and fortune, and his dearest affections, at its shrine. The sacrifice was demanded from, and made by, a youth of seventeen. It is a singular fact in the history of society in the civilized nations of modern times that no false step is so irretrievable as one made in early youth. Older men, it is true, when they oppose their fellows and transgress ordinary rules, carry a certain prudence or hypocrisy as a shield along with them. But youth is rash; nor can it imagine, while asserting what it believes to be true, and doing what it believes to be right, that it should be denounced as vicious, and pursued as a criminal.

Shelley possessed a quality of mind which experience has shown me to be of the rarest occurrence among human beings: this was his UNWORLDLI-NESS.
The usual motives that rule men, prospects of present or future advantage, the rank and fortune of those around, the taunts and censures, or the praise, of those who were hostile to him, had no influence whatever over his actions, and apparently none over his thoughts. It is difficult even to express the simplicity and directness of purpose that adorned him. Some few might be found in the history of mankind, and some one at least among his own friends, equally disinterested and scornful, even to severe personal sacrifices, of every baser motive. But no one, I believe, ever joined this noble but passive virtue to equal active endeavours for the benefit of his friends and mankind in general, and to equal power to produce the advantages he desired. The world's brightest gauds and its most solid advantages were of no worth in his eyes, when compared to the cause of what he considered truth, and the good of his fellow-creatures. Born in a position which, to his inexperienced mind, afforded the greatest facilities to practise the tenets he espoused, he boldly declared the use he would make of fortune and station, and enjoyed the belief that he should materially benefit his fellow-creatures by his actions; while, conscious of surpassing powers of reason and imagination, it is not strange that he should, even while so young, have believed that his

written thoughts would tend to disseminate opinions which he believed conducive to the happiness of the human race.

If man were a creature devoid of passion, he might have said and done all this with quietness. But he was too enthusiastic, and too full of hatred of all the ills he witnessed, not to scorn danger. Various disappointments tortured, but could not tame, his soul. The more enmity he met, the more earnestly he became attached to his peculiar views, and hostile to those of the men who persecuted him.

He was animated to greater zeal by compassion for his fellow-creatures. His sympathy was excited by the misery with which the world is burning. He witnessed the sufferings of the poor, and was aware of the evils of ignorance. He desired to induce every rich man to despoil himself of superfluity, and to create a brotherhood of property and service, and was ready to be the first to lay down the advantages of his birth. He was of too uncompromising a disposition to join any party. He did not in his youth look forward to gradual improvement: nay, in those days of intolerance, now almost forgotten, it seemed as easy to look forward to the sort of millennium of freedom and brotherhood which he thought the proper state of mankind as to the present reign of moderation and improvement. Ill-health made him believe that his race would soon be run; that a year or two was all he had of life. He desired that these years should be useful and illustrious. He saw, in a fervent call on his fellow-creatures to share alike the blessings of the creation, to love and serve each other, the noblest work that life and time permitted him. In this spirit he composed "Queen Mab".

He was a lover of the wonderful and wild in literature, but had not fostered these tastes at their genuine sources--the romances and chivalry of the middle ages--but in the perusal of such German works as were current in those days. Under the influence of these he, at the age of fifteen, wrote two short prose romances of slender merit. The sentiments and language were exaggerated, the composition imitative and poor. He wrote also a poem on the subject of Ahasuerus--being led to it by a German fragment he picked up, dirty and torn, in Lincoln's Inn Fields. This fell afterwards into other hands, and was considerably altered before it was printed. Our earlier English poetry was almost unknown to him. The love and knowledge of Nature developed by Wordsworth--the lofty melody and mysterious beauty of Coleridge's poetry--and the wild fantastic machinery and gorgeous scenery adopted by Southey--composed his favourite reading; the rhythm of "Queen Mab" was founded on that of "Thalaba", and the first few lines bear a striking resemblance in spirit, though not in idea, to the opening of that poem. His fertile imagination, and ear tuned to the finest sense of harmony, preserved him from imitation. Another of his favourite books was the poem of "Gebir" by Walter Savage Landor. From his boyhood he had a wonderful facility of versification, which he carried into another language; and his Latin school-verses were composed with an ease and correctness that procured for him prizes, and caused him to be resorted to by all his friends for help. He was, at the period of writing "Queen Mab", a great traveller within the limits of England, Scotland, and Ireland. His time was spent among the loveliest scenes of these countries. Mountain and lake and forest were his home; the phenomena of Nature were his favourite study. He loved to inquire into their causes, and was addicted to pursuits of natural philosophy and chemistry, as far as they could be carried on as an amusement. These tastes gave truth and vivacity to his descriptions, and warmed his soul with that deep admiration for the wonders of Nature which constant association with her inspired.

He never intended to publish "Queen Mab" as it stands; but a few years after, when printing "Alastor", he extracted a small portion which he entitled "The Daemon of the World". In this he changed somewhat the versification, and made other alterations scarcely to be called improvements.

Some years after, when in Italy, a bookseller published an edition of "Queen Mab" as it originally stood. Shelley was hastily written to by his friends, under the idea that, deeply injurious as the mere distribution of the poem had proved, the publication might awaken fresh persecutions. At the suggestion of these friends he wrote a letter on the subject, printed in the "Examiner" newspaper--with which I close this history of his earliest work.

TO THE EDITOR OF THE 'EXAMINER.'

'Sir,

'Having heard that a poem entitled "Queen Mab" has been surreptitiously published in London, and that legal proceedings have been instituted against the publisher, I request the favour of your insertion of the following explanation of the affair, as it relates to me.

'A poem entitled "Queen Mab" was written by me at the age of eighteen, I daresay in a sufficiently intemperate spirit--but even then was not intended for publication, and a few copies only were struck off, to be distributed among my personal friends. I have not seen this production for several years. I doubt not but that it is perfectly worthless in point of literary composition; and that, in all that concerns moral and political speculation, as well as in the subtler discriminations of metaphysical and religious doctrine, it is still more crude and immature. I am a devoted enemy to religious, political, and domestic oppression; and I regret this publication, not so much from literary vanity, as because I fear it is better fitted to injure than to serve the sacred cause of freedom. I have directed my solicitor to apply to Chancery for an injunction to restrain the sale; but, after the precedent of Mr. Southey's "Wat Tyler" (a poem written, I believe, at the same age, and with the same unreflecting enthusiasm), with little hope of success.

'Whilst I exonerate myself from all share in having divulged opinions hostile to existing sanctions, under the form, whatever it may be, which they assume in this poem, it is scarcely necessary for me to protest against the system of inculcating the truth of Christianity or the excellence of Monarchy, however true or however excellent they may be, by such equivocal arguments as confiscation and imprisonment, and invective and slander, and the insolent violation of the most sacred ties of Nature and society.

'SIR,

'I am your obliged and obedient servant,

'PERCY B. SHELLEY.

'Pisa, June 22, 1821.'

NOTE ON "ALASTOR", BY MRS. SHELLEY.

"Alastor" is written in a very different tone from "Queen Mab". In the latter, Shelley poured out all the cherished speculations of his youth--all the irrepressible emotions of sympathy, censure, and hope, to which the present suffering, and what he considers the proper destiny of his fellow-creatures, gave birth. "Alastor", on the contrary, contains an individual interest only. A very few years, with their attendant events, had checked the ardour of Shelley's hopes, though he still thought them well-grounded, and that to advance their fulfilment was the noblest task man could achieve.

This is neither the time nor place to speak of the misfortunes that chequered his life. It will be sufficient to say that, in all he did, he

at the time of doing it believed himself justified to his own
conscience; while the various ills of poverty and loss of friends
brought home to him the sad realities of life. Physical suffering had
also considerable influence in causing him to turn his eyes inward;
inclining him rather to brood over the thoughts and emotions of his own
soul than to glance abroad, and to make, as in "Queen Mab", the whole
universe the object and subject of his song. In the Spring of
1815, an eminent physician pronounced that he was dying rapidly of a
consumption; abscesses were formed on his lungs, and he suffered acute
spasms. Suddenly a complete change took place; and though through life
he was a martyr to pain and debility, every symptom of pulmonary disease
vanished. His nerves, which nature had formed sensitive to an unexampled
degree, were rendered still more susceptible by the state of his health.

As soon as the peace of 1814 had opened the Continent, he went abroad.
He visited some of the more magnificent scenes of Switzerland, and
returned to England from Lucerne, by the Reuss and the Rhine. The
river-navigation enchanted him. In his favourite poem of "Thalaba", his
imagination had been excited by a description of such a voyage. In the
summer of 1815, after a tour along the southern coast of Devonshire and
a visit to Clifton, he rented a house on Bishopsgate Heath, on the
borders of Windsor Forest, where he enjoyed several months of
comparative health and tranquil happiness. The later summer months were
warm and dry. Accompanied by a few friends, he visited the source of the
Thames, making a voyage in a wherry from Windsor to Crichlade. His
beautiful stanzas in the churchyard of Lechlade were written on that
occasion. "Alastor" was composed on his return. He spent his days under
the oak-shades of Windsor Great Park; and the magnificent woodland was a
fitting study to inspire the various descriptions of forest scenery we
find in the poem.

None of Shelley's poems is more characteristic than this. The solemn
spirit that reigns throughout, the worship of the majesty of nature, the

broodings of a poet's heart in solitude--the mingling of the exulting joy which the various aspects of the visible universe inspires with the sad and struggling pangs which human passion imparts--give a touching interest to the whole. The death which he had often contemplated during the last months as certain and near he here represented in such colours as had, in his lonely musings, soothed his soul to peace. The versification sustains the solemn spirit which breathes throughout: it is peculiarly melodious. The poem ought rather to be considered didactic than narrative: it was the outpouring of his own emotions, embodied in the purest form he could conceive, painted in the ideal hues which his brilliant imagination inspired, and softened by the recent anticipation of death.

NOTE ON THE "REVOLT OF ISLAM", BY MRS. SHELLEY.

Shelley possessed two remarkable qualities of intellect--a brilliant imagination, and a logical exactness of reason. His inclinations led him (he fancied) almost alike to poetry and metaphysical discussions. I say 'he fancied,' because I believe the former to have been paramount, and that it would have gained the mastery even had he struggled against it. However, he said that he deliberated at one time whether he should dedicate himself to poetry or metaphysics; and, resolving on the former, he educated himself for it, discarding in a great measure his philosophical pursuits, and engaging himself in the study of the poets of Greece, Italy, and England. To these may be added a constant perusal of portions of the old Testament--the Psalms, the Book of Job, the Prophet Isaiah, and others, the sublime poetry of which filled him with delight.

As a poet, his intellect and compositions were powerfully influenced by exterior circumstances, and especially by his place of abode. He was very fond of travelling, and ill-health increased this restlessness. The sufferings occasioned by a cold English winter made him pine, especially when our colder spring arrived, for a more genial climate. In 1816 he again visited Switzerland, and rented a house on the banks of the Lake of Geneva; and many a day, in cloud or sunshine, was passed alone in his boat--sailing as the wind listed, or weltering on the calm waters. The majestic aspect of Nature ministered such thoughts as he afterwards enwove in verse. His lines on the Bridge of the Arve, and his "Hymn to Intellectual Beauty", were written at this time. Perhaps during this summer his genius was checked by association with another poet whose nature was utterly dissimilar to his own, yet who, in the poem he wrote at that time, gave tokens that he shared for a period the more abstract and etherealised inspiration of Shelley. The saddest events awaited his return to England; but such was his fear to wound the feelings of others that he never expressed the anguish he felt, and seldom gave vent to the indignation roused by the persecutions he underwent; while the course of deep unexpressed passion, and the sense of injury, engendered the desire to embody themselves in forms defecated of all the weakness and evil which cling to real life.

He chose therefore for his hero a youth nourished in dreams of liberty, some of whose actions are in direct opposition to the opinions of the world; but who is animated throughout by an ardent love of virtue, and a resolution to confer the boons of political and intellectual freedom on his fellow-creatures. He created for this youth a woman such as he delighted to imagine--full of enthusiasm for the same objects; and they both, with will unvanquished, and the deepest sense of the justice of their cause, met adversity and death. There exists in this poem a memorial of a friend of his youth. The character of the old man who liberates Laon from his tower prison, and tends on him in sickness, is founded on that of Doctor Lind, who, when Shelley was at Eton, had often stood by to befriend and support him, and whose name he never mentioned without love and veneration.

During the year 1817 we were established at Marlow in Buckinghamshire. Shelley's choice of abode was fixed chiefly by this town being at no great distance from London, and its neighbourhood to the Thames. The poem was written in his boat, as it floated under the beech groves of Bisham, or during wanderings in the neighbouring country, which is distinguished for peculiar beauty. The chalk hills break into cliffs that overhang the Thames, or form valleys clothed with beech; the wilder portion of the country is rendered beautiful by exuberant vegetation; and the cultivated part is peculiarly fertile. With all this wealth of Nature which, either in the form of gentlemen's parks or soil dedicated to agriculture, flourishes around, Marlow was inhabited (I hope it is altered now) by a very poor population. The women are lacemakers, and lose their health by sedentary labour, for which they were very ill paid. The Poor-laws ground to the dust not only the paupers, but those who had risen just above that state, and were obliged to pay poor-rates. The changes produced by peace following a long war, and a bad harvest, brought with them the most heart-rending evils to the poor. Shelley afforded what alleviation he could. In the winter, while bringing out his poem, he had a severe attack of ophthalmia, caught while visiting the poor cottages. I mention these things,--for this minute and active sympathy with his fellow-creatures gives a thousandfold interest to his speculations, and stamps with reality his pleadings for the human race.

The poem, bold in its opinions and uncompromising in their expression, met with many censurers, not only among those who allow of no virtue but such as supports the cause they espouse, but even among those whose opinions were similar to his own. I extract a portion of a letter written in answer to one of these friends. It best details the impulses of Shelley's mind, and his motives: it was written with entire unreserve; and is therefore a precious monument of his own opinion of his powers, of the purity of his designs, and the ardour with which he clung, in adversity and through the valley of the shadow of death, to views from which he believed the permanent happiness of mankind must eventually spring.

'Marlowe, December 11, 1817.

'I have read and considered all that you say about my general powers, and the particular instance of the poem in which I have attempted to develop them. Nothing can be more satisfactory to me than the interest which your admonitions express. But I think you are mistaken in some points with regard to the peculiar nature of my powers, whatever be their amount. I listened with deference and self-suspicion to your censures of "The Revolt of Islam"; but the productions of mine which you commend hold a very low place in my own esteem; and this reassures me, in some degree at least. The poem was produced by a series of thoughts which filled my mind with unbounded and sustained enthusiasm. I felt the precariousness of my life, and I engaged in this task, resolved to leave some record of myself. Much of what the volume contains was written with the same feeling--as real, though not so prophetic--as the communications of a dying man. I never presumed indeed to consider it anything approaching to faultless; but, when I consider contemporary productions of the same apparent pretensions, I own I was filled with confidence. I felt that it was in many respects a genuine picture of my own mind. I felt that the sentiments were true, not assumed. And in this have I long believed that my power consists; in sympathy, and that part of the imagination which relates to sentiment and contemplation. I am formed, if for anything not in common with the herd of mankind, to apprehend minute and remote distinctions of feeling, whether relative to external nature or the living beings which surround us, and to communicate the conceptions which result from considering either the moral or the material universe as a whole. Of course, I believe these faculties, which perhaps comprehend all that is sublime in man, to exist very imperfectly in my own mind. But, when you advert to my Chancery-paper, a cold, forced, unimpassioned, insignificant piece of cramped and cautious argument, and to the little scrap about "Mandeville", which expressed my feelings indeed, but cost scarcely two minutes' thought to express, as specimens of my powers more favourable than that which grew as it were from "the agony and bloody sweat" of intellectual travail; surely I must feel that, in some manner, either I am mistaken in believing that I have any talent at all, or you in the selection of the specimens of it. Yet, after all, I cannot but be conscious, in much of what I write, of an absence of that tranquillity which is the attribute and accompaniment of power. This feeling alone would make your most kind and wise admonitions, on the subject of the economy of intellectual force, valuable to me. And, if I live, or if I see any trust in coming years, doubt not but that I shall do something, whatever it may be, which a serious and earnest estimate of my powers will suggest to me, and which will be in every respect accommodated to their utmost limits.

[Shelley to Godwin.]

NOTE ON ROSALIND AND HELEN
BY MRS. SHELLEY.

"Rosalind and Helen" was begun at Marlow, and thrown aside--till I found it; and, at my request, it was completed. Shelley had no care for any of his poems that did not emanate from the depths of his mind, and develop some high or abstruse truth. When he does touch on human life and the human heart, no pictures can be more faithful, more delicate, more subtle, or more pathetic. He never mentioned Love but he shed a grace borrowed from his own nature, that scarcely any other poet has bestowed on that passion. When he spoke of it as the law of life, which inasmuch as we rebel against we err and injure ourselves and others, he promulgated that which he considered an irrefragable truth. In his eyes it was the essence of our being, and all woe and pain arose from the war made against it by selfishness, or insensibility, or mistake. By reverting in his mind to this first principle, he discovered the source of many emotions, and could disclose the secrets of all hearts, and his delineations of passion and emotion touch the finest chords of our nature.

"Rosalind and Helen" was finished during the summer of 1818, while we were at the Baths of Lucca.

NOTE BY MRS. SHELLEY.

From the Baths of Lucca, in 1818, Shelley visited Venice; and, circumstances rendering it eligible that we should remain a few weeks in the neighbourhood of that city, he accepted the offer of Lord Byron, who lent him the use of a villa he rented near Este; and he sent for his family from Lucca to join him.

I Capuccini was a villa built on the site of a Capuchin convent, demolished when the French suppressed religious houses; it was situated on the very overhanging brow of a low hill at the foot of a range of higher ones. The house was cheerful and pleasant; a vine-trellised walk, a pergola, as it is called in Italian, led from the hall-door to a summer-house at the end of the garden, which Shelley made his study, and in which he began the "Prometheus"; and here also, as he mentions in a letter, he wrote "Julian and Maddalo". A slight ravine, with a road in its depth, divided the garden from the hill, on which stood the ruins of the ancient castle of Este, whose dark massive wall gave forth an echo, and from whose ruined crevices owls and bats flitted forth at night, as the crescent moon sunk behind the black and heavy battlements. We looked from the garden over the wide plain of Lombardy, bounded to the west by the far Apennines, while to the east the horizon was lost in misty distance. After the picturesque but limited view of mountain, ravine, and chestnut-wood, at the Baths of Lucca, there was something infinitely gratifying to the eye in the wide range of prospect commanded by our new abode.

Our first misfortune, of the kind from which we soon suffered even more severely, happened here. Our little girl, an infant in whose small features I fancied that I traced great resemblance to her father, showed symptoms of suffering from the heat of the climate. Teething increased her illness and danger. We were at Este, and when we became alarmed, hastened to Venice for the best advice. When we arrived at Fusina, we found that we had forgotten our passport, and the soldiers on duty attempted to prevent our crossing the laguna; but they could not resist Shelley's impetuosity at such a moment. We had scarcely arrived at Venice before life fled from the little sufferer, and we returned to Este to weep her loss.

After a few weeks spent in this retreat, which was interspersed by visits to Venice, we proceeded southward.

NOTE ON "PROMETHEUS UNBOUND", BY MRS. SHELLEY.

On the 12th of March, 1818, Shelley quitted England, never to return. His principal motive was the hope that his health would be improved by a milder climate; he suffered very much during the winter previous to his emigration, and this decided his vacillating purpose. In December, 1817, he had written from Marlow to a friend, saying:

'My health has been materially worse. My feelings at intervals are of a deadly and torpid kind, or awakened to such a state of unnatural and keen excitement that, only to instance the organ of sight, I find the very blades of grass and the boughs of distant trees present themselves to me with microscopic distinctness. Towards evening I sink into a state of lethargy and inanimation, and often remain for hours on the sofa between sleep and waking, a prey to the most painful irritability of thought. Such, with little intermission, is my condition. The hours devoted to study are selected with vigilant caution from among these periods of endurance. It is not for this that I think of travelling to Italy, even if I knew that Italy would relieve me. But I have experienced a decisive pulmonary attack; and although at present it has passed away without any considerable vestige of its existence, yet this symptom sufficiently shows the true nature of my disease to be consumptive. It is to my advantage that this malady is in its nature slow, and, if one is sufficiently alive to its advances, is susceptible of cure from a warm climate. In the event of its assuming any decided shape, IT WOULD BE MY DUTY to go to Italy without delay. It is not mere health, but life, that I should seek, and that not for my own sake--I feel I am capable of trampling on all such weakness; but for the sake of those to whom my life may be a source of happiness, utility, security, and honour, and to some of whom my death might be all that is the reverse.'

In almost every respect his journey to Italy was advantageous. He left behind friends to whom he was attached; but cares of a thousand kinds, many springing from his lavish generosity, crowded round him in his native country, and, except the society of one or two friends, he had no compensation. The climate caused him to consume half his existence in helpless suffering. His dearest pleasure, the free enjoyment of the scenes of Nature, was marred by the same circumstance.

He went direct to Italy, avoiding even Paris, and did not make any pause till he arrived at Milan. The first aspect of Italy enchanted Shelley; it seemed a garden of delight placed beneath a clearer and brighter heaven than any he had lived under before. He wrote long descriptive letters during the first year of his residence in Italy, which, as compositions, are the most beautiful in the world, and show how truly he appreciated and studied the wonders of Nature and Art in that divine land.

The poetical spirit within him speedily revived with all the power and with more than all the beauty of his first attempts. He meditated three subjects as the groundwork for lyrical dramas. One was the story of Tasso; of this a slight fragment of a song of Tasso remains. The other was one founded on the Book of Job, which he never abandoned in idea, but of which no trace remains among his papers. The third was the "Prometheus Unbound". The Greek tragedians were now his most familiar companions in his wanderings, and the sublime majesty of Aeschylus filled him with wonder and delight. The father of Greek tragedy does not possess the pathos of Sophocles, nor the variety and tenderness of Euripides; the interest on which he founds his dramas is often elevated above human vicissitudes into the mighty passions and throes of gods and demi-gods: such fascinated the abstract imagination of Shelley.

We spent a month at Milan, visiting the Lake of Como during that interval. Thence we passed in succession to Pisa, Leghorn, the Baths of Lucca, Venice, Este, Rome, Naples, and back again to Rome, whither we returned early in March, 1819. During all this time Shelley meditated the subject of his drama, and wrote portions of it. Other poems were composed during this interval, and while at the Bagni di Lucca he translated Plato's "Symposium". But, though he diversified his studies, his thoughts centred in the Prometheus. At last, when at Rome, during a bright and beautiful Spring, he gave up his whole time to the composition. The spot selected for his study was, as he mentions in his preface, the mountainous ruins of the Baths of Caracalla. These are little known to the ordinary visitor at Rome. He describes them in a letter, with that poetry and delicacy and truth of description which render his narrated impressions of scenery of unequalled beauty and interest.

At first he completed the drama in three acts. It was not till several months after, when at Florence, that he conceived that a fourth act, a sort of hymn of rejoicing in the fulfilment of the prophecies with regard to Prometheus, ought to be added to complete the composition.

The prominent feature of Shelley's theory of the destiny of the human species was that evil is not inherent in the system of the creation, but an accident that might be expelled. This also forms a portion of Christianity: God made earth and man perfect, till he, by his fall,

   'Brought death into the world and all our woe.'

Shelley believed that mankind had only to will that there should be no evil, and there would be none. It is not my part in these Notes to notice the arguments that have been urged against this opinion, but to mention the fact that he entertained it, and was indeed attached to it with fervent enthusiasm. That man could be so perfectionized as to be able to expel evil from his own nature, and from the greater part of the creation, was the cardinal point of his system. And the subject he loved best to dwell on was the image of One warring with the Evil Principle, oppressed not only by it, but by all--even the good, who were deluded into considering evil a necessary portion of humanity; a victim full of fortitude and hope and the spirit of triumph emanating from a reliance in the ultimate omnipotence of Good. Such he had depicted in his last poem, when he made Laon the enemy and the victim of tyrants. He now took a more idealized image of the same subject. He followed certain classical authorities in figuring Saturn as the good principle, Jupiter the usurping evil one, and Prometheus as the regenerator, who, unable to bring mankind back to primitive innocence, used knowledge as a weapon to defeat evil, by leading mankind, beyond the state wherein they are sinless through ignorance, to that in which they are virtuous through wisdom. Jupiter punished the temerity of the Titan by chaining him to a rock of Caucasus, and causing a vulture to devour his still-renewed heart. There was a prophecy afloat in heaven portending the fall of Jove, the secret of averting which was known only to Prometheus; and the god offered freedom from torture on condition of its being communicated to him. According to the mythological story, this referred to the offspring of Thetis, who was destined to be greater than his father. Prometheus at last bought pardon for his crime of enriching mankind with his gifts, by revealing the prophecy. Hercules killed the vulture, and set him free; and Thetis was married to Peleus, the father of Achilles.

Shelley adapted the catastrophe of this story to his peculiar views. The son greater than his father, born of the nuptials of Jupiter and Thetis, was to dethrone Evil, and bring back a happier reign than that of Saturn. Prometheus defies the power of his enemy, and endures centuries of torture; till the hour arrives when Jove, blind to the real event, but darkly guessing that some great good to himself will flow, espouses Thetis. At the moment, the Primal Power of the world drives him from his usurped throne, and Strength, in the person of Hercules, liberates Humanity, typified in Prometheus, from the tortures generated by evil done or suffered. Asia, one of the Oceanides, is the wife of Prometheus--she was, according to other mythological interpretations, the same as Venus and Nature. When the benefactor of mankind is liberated, Nature resumes the beauty of her prime, and is united to her husband, the emblem of the human race, in perfect and happy union. In the Fourth Act, the Poet gives further scope to his imagination, and idealizes the forms of creation--such as we know them, instead of such as they appeared to the Greeks. Maternal Earth, the mighty parent, is superseded by the Spirit of the Earth, the guide of our planet through the realms of sky; while his fair and weaker companion and attendant, the Spirit of the Moon, receives bliss from the annihilation of Evil in the superior sphere.

Shelley develops, more particularly in the lyrics of this drama, his abstruse and imaginative theories with regard to the Creation. It requires a mind as subtle and penetrating as his own to understand the mystic meanings scattered throughout the poem. They elude the ordinary reader by their abstraction and delicacy of distinction, but they are far from vague. It was his design to write prose metaphysical essays on the nature of Man, which would have served to explain much of what is obscure in his poetry; a few scattered fragments of observations and remarks alone remain. He considered these philosophical views of Mind and Nature to be instinct with the intensest spirit of poetry.

More popular poets clothe the ideal with familiar and sensible imagery. Shelley loved to idealize the real--to gift the mechanism of the material universe with a soul and a voice, and to bestow such also on the most delicate and abstract emotions and thoughts of the mind. Sophocles was his great master in this species of imagery.

I find in one of his manuscript books some remarks on a line in the "Oedipus Tyrannus", which show at once the critical subtlety of Shelley's mind, and explain his apprehension of those 'minute and remote distinctions of feeling, whether relative to external nature or the living beings which surround us,' which he pronounces, in the letter quoted in the note to the "Revolt of Islam", to comprehend all that is sublime in man.

'In the Greek Shakespeare, Sophocles, we find the image,

  Pollas d' odous elthonta phrontidos planois:

a line of almost unfathomable depth of poetry; yet how simple are the images in which it is arrayed!

"Coming to many ways in the wanderings of careful thought."

If the words odous and planois had not been used, the line might have been explained in a metaphorical instead of an absolute sense, as we say "WAYS and means," and "wanderings" for error and confusion. But they meant literally paths or roads, such as we tread with our feet; and wanderings, such as a man makes when he loses himself in a desert, or roams from city to city--as Oedipus, the speaker of this verse, was destined to wander, blind and asking charity. What a picture does this line suggest of the mind as a wilderness of intricate paths, wide as the universe, which is here made its symbol; a world within a world which he who seeks some knowledge with respect to what he ought to do searches throughout, as he would search the external universe for some valued thing which was hidden from him upon its surface.'

In reading Shelley's poetry, we often find similar verses, resembling, but not imitating the Greek in this species of imagery; for, though he adopted the style, he gifted it with that originality of form and colouring which sprung from his own genius.

In the "Prometheus Unbound", Shelley fulfils the promise quoted from a letter in the Note on the "Revolt of Islam". (While correcting the proof-sheets of that poem, it struck me that the poet had indulged in an exaggerated view of the evils of restored despotism; which, however injurious and degrading, were less openly sanguinary than the triumph of anarchy, such as it appeared in France at the close of the last century. But at this time a book, "Scenes of Spanish Life", translated by Lieutenant Crawford from the German of Dr. Huber, of Rostock, fell into my hands. The account of the triumph of the priests and the serviles, after the French invasion of Spain in 1823, bears a strong and frightful resemblance to some of the descriptions of the massacre of the patriots in the "Revolt of Islam".) The tone of the composition is calmer and more majestic, the poetry more perfect as a whole, and the imagination displayed at once more pleasingly beautiful and more varied and daring. The description of the Hours, as they are seen in the cave of Demogorgon, is an instance of this--it fills the mind as the most charming picture--we long to see an artist at work to bring to our view the

'cars drawn by rainbow-winged steeds
Which trample the dim winds: in each there stands
A wild-eyed charioteer urging their flight.
Some look behind, as fiends pursued them there,
And yet I see no shapes but the keen stars:
Others, with burning eyes, lean forth, and drink
With eager lips the wind of their own speed,
As if the thing they loved fled on before,
And now, even now, they clasped it. Their bright locks
Stream like a comet's flashing hair: they all
Sweep onward.'

Through the whole poem there reigns a sort of calm and holy spirit of love; it soothes the tortured, and is hope to the expectant, till the prophecy is fulfilled, and Love, untainted by any evil, becomes the law of the world.

England had been rendered a painful residence to Shelley, as much by the sort of persecution with which in those days all men of liberal opinions were visited, and by the injustice he had lately endured in the Court of Chancery, as by the symptoms of disease which made him regard a visit to Italy as necessary to prolong his life. An exile, and strongly impressed with the feeling that the majority of his countrymen regarded him with sentiments of aversion such as his own heart could experience towards none, he sheltered himself from such disgusting and painful thoughts in the calm retreats of poetry, and built up a world of his own--with the more pleasure, since he hoped to induce some one or two to believe that the earth might become such, did mankind themselves consent. The charm of the Roman climate helped to clothe his thoughts in greater beauty than they had ever worn before. And, as he wandered among the ruins made one with Nature in their decay, or gazed on the Praxitelean shapes that throng the Vatican, the Capitol, and the palaces of Rome, his soul imbibed forms of loveliness which became a portion of itself. There are many passages in the "Prometheus" which show the intense delight he received from such studies, and give back the impression with a beauty of poetical description peculiarly his own. He felt this, as a poet must feel when he satisfies himself by the result of his labours; and he wrote from Rome, 'My "Prometheus Unbound" is just finished, and in a month or two I shall send it. It is a drama, with characters and mechanism of a kind yet unattempted; and I think the execution is better than any of my former attempts.'

I may mention, for the information of the more critical reader, that the verbal alterations in this edition of "Prometheus" are made from a list of errata written by Shelley himself.

NOTE ON THE CENCI, BY MRS. SHELLEY.

The sort of mistake that Shelley made as to the extent of his own genius and powers, which led him deviously at first, but lastly into the direct track that enabled him fully to develop them, is a curious instance of his modesty of feeling, and of the methods which the human mind uses at once to deceive itself, and yet, in its very delusion, to make its way out of error into the path which Nature has marked out as its right one. He often incited me to attempt the writing a tragedy: he conceived that I possessed some dramatic talent, and he was always most earnest and energetic in his exhortations that I should cultivate any talent I possessed, to the utmost. I entertained a truer estimate of my powers; and above all (though at that time not exactly aware of the fact) I was far too young to have any chance of succeeding, even moderately, in a species of composition that requires a greater scope of experience in, and sympathy with, human passion than could then have fallen to my lot,--or than any perhaps, except Shelley, ever possessed, even at the age of twenty-six, at which he wrote The Cenci.

On the other hand, Shelley most erroneously conceived himself to be destitute of this talent. He believed that one of the first requisites was the capacity of forming and following-up a story or plot. He fancied himself to he defective in this portion of imagination: it was that which gave him least pleasure in the writings of others, though he laid great store by it as the proper framework to support the sublimest efforts of poetry. He asserted that he was too metaphysical and abstract, too fond of the theoretical and the ideal, to succeed as a tragedian. It perhaps is not strange that I shared this opinion with himself; for he had hitherto shown no inclination for, nor given any specimen of his powers in framing and supporting the interest of a story, either in prose or verse. Once or twice, when he attempted such, he had speedily thrown it aside, as being even disagreeable to him as an occupation.

The subject he had suggested for a tragedy was Charles I: and he had written to me: 'Remember, remember Charles I. I have been already imagining how you would conduct some scenes. The second volume of "St. Leon" begins with this proud and true sentiment: "There is nothing which the human mind can conceive which it may not execute." Shakespeare was only a human being.' These words were written in 1818, while we were in Lombardy, when he little thought how soon a work of his own would prove a proud comment on the passage he quoted. When in Rome, in 1819, a friend put into our hands the old manuscript account of the story of the Cenci. We visited the Colonna and Doria palaces, where the portraits of Beatrice were to be found; and her beauty cast the reflection of its own grace over her appalling story. Shelley's imagination became strongly excited, and he urged the subject to me as one fitted for a tragedy. More than ever I felt my incompetence; but I entreated him to write it instead; and he began, and proceeded swiftly, urged on by intense sympathy with the sufferings of the human beings whose passions, so long cold in the tomb, he revived, and gifted with poetic language. This tragedy is the only one of his works that he communicated to me during its progress. We talked over the arrangement of the scenes together. I speedily saw the great mistake we had made, and triumphed in the discovery of the new talent brought to light from that mine of wealth (never, alas, through his untimely death, worked to its depths)--his richly gifted mind.

We suffered a severe affliction in Rome by the loss of our eldest child, who was of such beauty and promise as to cause him deservedly to be the idol of our hearts. We left the capital of the world, anxious for a time to escape a spot associated too intimately with his presence and loss. (Such feelings haunted him when, in "The Cenci", he makes Beatrice speak to Cardinal Camillo of

 'that fair blue-eyed child
Who was the lodestar of your life:'--and say--
All see, since his most swift and piteous death,
That day and night, and heaven and earth, and time,
And all the things hoped for or done therein
Are changed to you, through your exceeding grief.')

Some friends of ours were residing in the neighbourhood of Leghorn, and we took a small house, Villa Valsovano, about half-way between the town and Monte Nero, where we remained during the summer. Our villa was situated in the midst of a podere; the peasants sang as they worked beneath our windows, during the heats of a very hot season, and in the evening the water-wheel creaked as the process of irrigation went on, and the fireflies flashed from among the myrtle hedges: Nature was bright, sunshiny, and cheerful, or diversified by storms of a majestic terror, such as we had never before witnessed.

At the top of the house there was a sort of terrace. There is often such in Italy, generally roofed: this one was very small, yet not only roofed but glazed. This Shelley made his study; it looked out on a wide prospect of fertile country, and commanded a view of the near sea. The storms that sometimes varied our day showed themselves most picturesquely as they were driven across the ocean; sometimes the dark lurid clouds dipped towards the waves, and became water-spouts that churned up the waters beneath, as they were chased onward and scattered by the tempest. At other times the dazzling sunlight and heat made it almost intolerable to every other; but Shelley basked in both, and his health and spirits revived under their influence. In this airy cell he wrote the principal part of "The Cenci". He was making a study of Calderon at the time, reading his best tragedies with an accomplished lady living near us, to whom his letter from Leghorn was addressed during the following year. He admired Calderon, both for his poetry and his dramatic genius; but it shows his judgement and originality that, though greatly struck by his first acquaintance with the Spanish poet, none of his peculiarities crept into the composition of "The Cenci"; and there is no trace of his new studies, except in that passage to which he himself alludes as suggested by one in "El Purgatorio de San Patricio".

Shelley wished "The Cenci" to be acted. He was not a playgoer, being of such fastidious taste that he was easily disgusted by the bad filling-up of the inferior parts. While preparing for our departure from England, however, he saw Miss O'Neil several times. She was then in the zenith of her glory; and Shelley was deeply moved by her impersonation of several parts, and by the graceful sweetness, the intense pathos, the sublime vehemence of passion she displayed. She was often in his thoughts as he wrote: and, when he had finished, he became anxious that his tragedy should be acted, and receive the advantage of having this accomplished actress to fill the part of the heroine. With this view he wrote the following letter to a friend in London:

'The object of the present letter us to ask a favour of you. I have written a tragedy on a story well known in Italy, and, in my conception, eminently dramatic. I have taken some pains to make my play fit for representation, and those who have already seen it judge favourably. It is written without any of the peculiar feelings and opinions which characterize my other compositions; I have attended simply to the impartial development of such characters as it is probable the persons represented really were, together with the greatest degree of popular effect to be produced by such a development. I send you a translation of the Italian manuscript on which my play is founded; the chief circumstance of which I have touched very delicately; for my principal doubt as to whether it would succeed as an acting play hangs entirely on the question as to whether any such a thing as incest in this shape, however treated, would be admitted on the stage. I think, however, it will form no objection; considering, first, that the facts are matter of history, and, secondly, the peculiar delicacy with which I have treated it. (In speaking of his mode of treating this main incident, Shelley said that it might be remarked that, in the course of the play, he had never mentioned expressly Cenci's worst crime. Every one knew what it must be, but it was never imaged in words--the nearest allusion to it being that portion of Cenci's curse beginning--"That, if she have a child," etc.)

'I am exceedingly interested in the question of whether this attempt of mine will succeed or not. I am strongly inclined to the affirmative at present; founding my hopes on this--that, as a composition, it is certainly not inferior to any of the modern plays that have been acted, with the exception of "Remorse"; that the interest of the plot is incredibly greater and more real; and that there is nothing beyond what the multitude are contented to believe that they can understand, either in imagery, opinion, or sentiment. I wish to preserve a complete incognito, and can trust to you that, whatever else you do, you will at least favour me on this point. Indeed, this is essential, deeply essential, to its success. After it had been acted, and successfully (could I hope for such a thing), I would own it if I pleased, and use the celebrity it might acquire to my own purposes.

'What I want you to do is to procure for me its presentation at Covent Garden. The principal character, Beatrice, is precisely fitted for Miss O'Neil, and it might even seem to have been written for her (God forbid that I should see her play it--it would tear my nerves to pieces); and in all respects it is fitted only for Covent Garden. The chief male character I confess I should be very unwilling that any one but Kean should play. That is impossible, and I must be contented with an inferior actor.'

The play was accordingly sent to Mr. Harris. He pronounced the subject to be so objectionable that he could not even submit the part to Miss O'Neil for perusal, but expressed his desire that the author would write a tragedy on some other subject, which he would gladly accept. Shelley printed a small edition at Leghorn, to ensure its correctness; as he was much annoyed by the many mistakes that crept into his text when distance prevented him from correcting the press.

Universal approbation soon stamped "The Cenci" as the best tragedy of modern times. Writing concerning it, Shelley said: 'I have been cautious to avoid the introducing faults of youthful composition; diffuseness, a profusion of inapplicable imagery, vagueness, generality, and, as Hamlet says, "words, words".' There is nothing that is not purely dramatic throughout; and the character of Beatrice, proceeding, from vehement struggle, to horror, to deadly resolution, and lastly to the elevated dignity of calm suffering, joined to passionate tenderness and pathos, is touched with hues so vivid and so beautiful that the poet seems to have read intimately the secrets of the noble heart imaged in the lovely countenance of the unfortunate girl. The Fifth Act is a masterpiece. It is the finest thing he ever wrote, and may claim proud comparison not only with any contemporary, but preceding, poet. The varying feelings of Beatrice are expressed with passionate, heart-reaching eloquence. Every character has a voice that echoes truth in its tones. It is curious, to one acquainted with the written story, to mark the success with which the poet has inwoven the real incidents of the tragedy into his scenes, and yet, through the power of poetry, has obliterated all that would otherwise have shown too harsh or too hideous in the picture. His success was a double triumph; and often after he was earnestly entreated to write again in a style that commanded popular favour, while it was not less instinct with truth and genius. But the bent of his mind went the other way; and, even when employed on subjects whose interest depended on character and incident, he would start off in another direction, and leave the delineations of human passion, which he could depict in so able a manner, for fantastic creations of his fancy, or the expression of those opinions and sentiments, with regard to human nature and its destiny, a desire to diffuse which was the master passion of his soul.

NOTE ON THE MASK OF ANARCHY, BY MRS. SHELLEY.

Though Shelley's first eager desire to excite his countrymen to resist openly the oppressions existent during 'the good old times' had faded with early youth, still his warmest sympathies were for the people. He was a republican, and loved a democracy. He looked on all human beings as inheriting an equal right to possess the dearest privileges of our nature; the necessaries of life when fairly earned by labour, and intellectual instruction. His hatred of any despotism that looked upon the people as not to be consulted, or protected from want and ignorance, was intense. He was residing near Leghorn, at Villa Valsovano, writing "The Cenci", when the news of the Manchester Massacre reached us; it roused in him violent emotions of indignation and compassion. The great truth that the many, if accordant and resolute, could control the few, as was shown some years after, made him long to teach his injured countrymen how to resist. Inspired by these feelings, he wrote the "Mask of Anarchy", which he sent to his friend Leigh Hunt, to be inserted in the Examiner, of which he was then the Editor.

'I did not insert it,' Leigh Hunt writes in his valuable and interesting preface to this poem, when he printed it in 1832, 'because I thought that the public at large had not become sufficiently discerning to do justice to the sincerity and kind-heartedness of the spirit that walked in this flaming robe of verse.' Days of outrage have passed away, and with them the exasperation that would cause such an appeal to the many to be injurious. Without being aware of them, they at one time acted on his suggestions, and gained the day. But they rose when human life was respected by the Minister in power; such was not the case during the Administration which excited Shelley's abhorrence.

The poem was written for the people, and is therefore in a more popular tone than usual: portions strike as abrupt and unpolished, but many stanzas are all his own. I heard him repeat, and admired, those beginning

   'My Father Time is old and gray,'

before I knew to what poem they were to belong. But the most touching passage is that which describes the blessed effects of liberty; it might make a patriot of any man whose heart was not wholly closed against his humbler fellow-creatures.

NOTE ON PETER BELL THE THIRD, BY MRS. SHELLEY.

In this new edition I have added "Peter Bell the Third". A critique on Wordsworth's "Peter Bell" reached us at Leghorn, which amused Shelley exceedingly, and suggested this poem.

I need scarcely observe that nothing personal to the author of "Peter Bell" is intended in this poem. No man ever admired Wordsworth's poetry more; --he read it perpetually, and taught others to appreciate its beauties. This poem is, like all others written by Shelley, ideal. He conceived the idealism of a poet--a man of lofty and creative genius--quitting the glorious calling of discovering and announcing the beautiful and good, to support and propagate ignorant prejudices and pernicious errors; imparting to the unenlightened, not that ardour for truth and spirit of toleration which Shelley looked on as the sources of the moral improvement and happiness of mankind, but false and injurious opinions, that evil was good, and that ignorance and force were the best allies of purity and virtue. His idea was that a man gifted, even as transcendently as the author of "Peter Bell", with the highest qualities of genius, must, if he fostered such errors, be infected with dulness. This poem was written as a warning--not as a narration of the reality. He was unacquainted personally with Wordsworth, or with Coleridge (to whom he alludes in the fifth part of the poem), and therefore, I repeat, his poem is purely ideal; --it contains something of criticism on the compositions of those great poets, but nothing injurious to the men themselves.

No poem contains more of Shelley's peculiar views with regard to the errors into which many of the wisest have fallen, and the pernicious effects of certain opinions on society. Much of it is beautifully written: and, though, like the burlesque drama of "Swellfoot", it must be looked on as a plaything, it has so much merit and poetry--so much of HIMSELF in it--that it cannot fail to interest greatly, and by right belongs to the world for whose instruction and benefit it was written.

NOTE ON THE WITCH OF ATLAS, BY MRS. SHELLEY.

We spent the summer of 1820 at the Baths of San Giuliano, four miles from Pisa. These baths were of great use to Shelley in soothing his nervous irritability. We made several excursions in the neighbourhood. The country around is fertile, and diversified and rendered picturesque by ranges of near hills and more distant mountains. The peasantry are a handsome intelligent race; and there was a gladsome sunny heaven spread over us, that rendered home and every scene we visited cheerful and bright. During some of the hottest days of August, Shelley made a solitary journey on foot to the summit of Monte San Pellegrino--a mountain of some height, on the top of which there is a chapel, the object, during certain days of the year, of many pilgrimages. The excursion delighted him while it lasted; though he exerted himself too much, and the effect was considerable lassitude and weakness on his return. During the expedition he conceived the idea, and wrote, in the three days immediately succeeding to his return, the "Witch of Atlas". This poem is peculiarly characteristic of his tastes--wildly fanciful, full of brilliant imagery, and discarding human interest and passion, to revel in the fantastic ideas that his imagination suggested.

The surpassing excellence of "The Cenci" had made me greatly desire that Shelley should increase his popularity by adopting subjects that would more suit the popular taste than a poem conceived in the abstract and dreamy spirit of the "Witch of Atlas". It was not only that I wished him to acquire popularity as redounding to his fame; but I believed that he would obtain a greater mastery over his own powers, and greater happiness in his mind, if public applause crowned his endeavours. The few stanzas that precede the poem were addressed to me on my representing these ideas to him. Even now I believe that I was in the right. Shelley did not expect sympathy and approbation from the public; but the want of it took away a portion of the ardour that ought to have sustained him while writing. He was thrown on his own resources, and on the inspiration of his own soul; and wrote because his mind overflowed, without the hope of being appreciated. I had not the most distant wish that he should truckle in opinion, or submit his lofty aspirations for the human race to the low ambition and pride of the many; but I felt sure that, if his poems were more addressed to the common feelings of men, his proper rank among the writers of the day would be acknowledged, and that popularity as a poet would enable his countrymen to do justice to his character and virtues, which in those days it was the mode to attack with the most flagitious calumnies and insulting abuse. That he felt these things deeply cannot be doubted, though he armed himself with the consciousness of acting from a lofty and heroic sense of right. The truth burst from his heart sometimes in solitude, and he would write a few unfinished verses that showed that he felt the sting; among such I find the following: --

> 'Alas! this is not what I thought Life was.
> I knew that there were crimes and evil men,
> Misery and hate; nor did I hope to pass
> Untouched by suffering through the rugged glen.
> In mine own heart I saw as in a glass
> The hearts of others...And, when
> I went among my kind, with triple brass
> Of calm endurance my weak breast I armed,
> To bear scorn, fear, and hate--a woful mass!'

I believed that all this morbid feeling would vanish if the chord of

sympathy between him and his countrymen were touched. But my persuasions
were vain, the mind could not be bent from its natural inclination.
Shelley shrunk instinctively from portraying human passion, with its
mixture of good and evil, of disappointment and disquiet. Such opened
again the wounds of his own heart; and he loved to shelter himself
rather in the airiest flights of fancy, forgetting love and hate, and
regret and lost hope, in such imaginations as borrowed their hues from
sunrise or sunset, from the yellow moonshine or paly twilight, from the
aspect of the far ocean or the shadows of the woods,--which celebrated
the singing of the winds among the pines, the flow of a murmuring
stream, and the thousand harmonious sounds which Nature creates in her
solitudes. These are the materials which form the "Witch of Atlas": it
is a brilliant congregation of ideas such as his senses gathered, and
his fancy coloured, during his rambles in the sunny land he so much
loved.

NOTE ON OEDIPUS TYRANNUS, BY MRS. SHELLEY.

In the brief journal I kept in those days, I find recorded, in August,
1820, Shelley 'begins "Swellfoot the Tyrant", suggested by the pigs at
the fair of San Giuliano.' This was the period of Queen Caroline's
landing in England, and the struggles made by George IV to get rid of
her claims; which failing, Lord Castlereagh placed the "Green Bag" on
the table of the House of Commons, demanding in the King's name that an
enquiry should be instituted into his wife's conduct. These
circumstances were the theme of all conversation among the English. We
were then at the Baths of San Giuliano. A friend came to visit us on the
day when a fair was held in the square, beneath our windows: Shelley
read to us his "Ode to Liberty"; and was riotously accompanied by the
grunting of a quantity of pigs brought for sale to the fair. He compared

it to the 'chorus of frogs' in the satiric drama of Aristophanes; and, it being an hour of merriment, and one ludicrous association suggesting another, he imagined a political-satirical drama on the circumstances of the day, to which the pigs would serve as chorus--and "Swellfoot" was begun. When finished, it was transmitted to England, printed, and published anonymously; but stifled at the very dawn of its existence by the Society for the Suppression of Vice, who threatened to prosecute it, if not immediately withdrawn. The friend who had taken the trouble of bringing it out, of course did not think it worth the annoyance and expense of a contest, and it was laid aside.

Hesitation of whether it would do honour to Shelley prevented my publishing it at first. But I cannot bring myself to keep back anything he ever wrote; for each word is fraught with the peculiar views and sentiments which he believed to be beneficial to the human race, and the bright light of poetry irradiates every thought. The world has a right to the entire compositions of such a man; for it does not live and thrive by the outworn lesson of the dullard or the hypocrite, but by the original free thoughts of men of genius, who aspire to pluck bright truth

> 'from the pale-faced moon;
> Or dive into the bottom of the deep
> Where fathom-line would never touch the ground,
> And pluck up drowned'

truth. Even those who may dissent from his opinions will consider that he was a man of genius, and that the world will take more interest in his slightest word than in the waters of Lethe which are so eagerly prescribed as medicinal for all its wrongs and woe. This drama, however, must not be judged for more than was meant. It is a mere plaything of the imagination; which even may not excite smiles among many, who will not see wit in those combinations of thought which were full of the ridiculous to the author. But, like everything he wrote, it breathes that deep sympathy for the sorrows of humanity, and indignation against its oppressors, which make it worthy of his name.

NOTE ON HELLAS, BY MRS. SHELLEY.

The South of Europe was in a state of great political excitement at the beginning of the year 1821. The Spanish Revolution had been a signal to Italy; secrete societies were formed; and, when Naples rose to declare the Constitution, the call was responded to from Brundusium to the foot of the Alps. To crush these attempts to obtain liberty, early in 1821 the Austrians poured their armies into the Peninsula: at first their coming rather seemed to add energy and resolution to a people long enslaved. The Piedmontese asserted their freedom; Genoa threw off the yoke of the King of Sardinia; and, as if in playful imitation, the people of the little state of Massa and Carrara gave the conge to their sovereign, and set up a republic.

Tuscany alone was perfectly tranquil. It was said that the Austrian minister presented a list of sixty Carbonari to the Grand Duke, urging their imprisonment; and the Grand Duke replied, 'I do not know whether these sixty men are Carbonari, but I know, if I imprison them, I shall directly have sixty thousand start up.' But, though the Tuscans had no desire to disturb the paternal government beneath whose shelter they slumbered, they regarded the progress of the various Italian revolutions with intense interest, and hatred for the Austrian was warm in every bosom. But they had slender hopes; they knew that the Neapolitans would offer no fit resistance to the regular German troops, and that the overthrow of the constitution in Naples would act as a decisive blow against all struggles for liberty in Italy.

We have seen the rise and progress of reform. But the Holy Alliance was alive and active in those days, and few could dream of the peaceful triumph of liberty. It seemed then that the armed assertion of freedom in the South of Europe was the only hope of the liberals, as, if it prevailed, the nations of the north would imitate the example. Happily the reverse has proved the fact. The countries accustomed to the exercise of the privileges of freemen, to a limited extent, have extended, and are extending, these limits. Freedom and knowledge have now a chance of proceeding hand in hand; and, if it continue thus, we may hope for the durability of both. Then, as I have said--in 1821--Shelley, as well as every other lover of liberty, looked upon the struggles in Spain and Italy as decisive of the destinies of the world, probably for centuries to come. The interest he took in the progress of affairs was intense. When Genoa declared itself free, his hopes were at their highest. Day after day he read the bulletins of the Austrian army, and sought eagerly to gather tokens of its defeat. He heard of the revolt of Genoa with emotions of transport. His whole heart and soul were in the triumph of the cause. We were living at Pisa at that time; and several well-informed Italians, at the head of whom we may place the celebrated Vacca, were accustomed to seek for sympathy in their hopes from Shelley: they did not find such for the despair they too generally experienced, founded on contempt for their southern countrymen.

While the fate of the progress of the Austrian armies then invading Naples was yet in suspense, the news of another revolution filled him with exultation. We had formed the acquaintance at Pisa of several Constantinopolitan Greeks, of the family of Prince Caradja, formerly Hospodar of Wallachia; who, hearing that the bowstring, the accustomed finale of his viceroyalty, was on the road to him, escaped with his treasures, and took up his abode in Tuscany. Among these was the gentleman to whom the drama of "Hellas" is dedicated. Prince Mavrocordato was warmed by those aspirations for the independence of his country which filled the hearts of many of his countrymen. He often intimated the possibility of an insurrection in Greece; but we had no idea of its being so near at hand, when, on the 1st of April 1821, he called on Shelley, bringing the proclamation of his cousin, Prince Ypsilanti, and, radiant with exultation and delight, declared that henceforth Greece would be free.

Shelley had hymned the dawn of liberty in Spain and Naples, in two odes dictated by the warmest enthusiasm; he felt himself naturally impelled to decorate with poetry the uprise of the descendants of that people whose works he regarded with deep admiration, and to adopt the vaticinatory character in prophesying their success. "Hellas" was written in a moment of enthusiasm. It is curious to remark how well he overcomes the difficulty of forming a drama out of such scant materials. His prophecies, indeed, came true in their general, not their particular, purport. He did not foresee the death of Lord Londonderry, which was to be the epoch of a change in English politics, particularly as regarded foreign affairs; nor that the navy of his country would fight for instead of against the Greeks, and by the battle of Navarino secure their enfranchisement from the Turks. Almost against reason, as it appeared to him, he resolved to believe that Greece would prove triumphant; and in this spirit, auguring ultimate good, yet grieving over the vicissitudes to be endured in the interval, he composed his drama.

"Hellas" was among the last of his compositions, and is among the most beautiful. The choruses are singularly imaginative, and melodious in their versification. There are some stanzas that beautifully exemplify Shelley's peculiar style; as, for instance, the assertion of the intellectual empire which must be for ever the inheritance of the country of Homer, Sophocles, and Plato:--

'But Greece and her foundations are
Built below the tide of war,
Based on the crystalline sea
Of thought and its eternity.'

And again, that philosophical truth felicitously imaged forth--

'Revenge and Wrong bring forth their kind,
The foul cubs like their parents are,
Their den is in the guilty mind,
And Conscience feeds them with despair.'

The conclusion of the last chorus is among the most beautiful of his lyrics. The imagery is distinct and majestic; the prophecy, such as poets love to dwell upon, the Regeneration of Mankind--and that regeneration reflecting back splendour on the foregone time, from which it inherits so much of intellectual wealth, and memory of past virtuous deeds, as must render the possession of happiness and peace of tenfold value.

NOTE ON THE EARLY POEMS, BY MRS. SHELLEY.

The remainder of Shelley's Poems will be arranged in the order in which they were written. Of course, mistakes will occur in placing some of the shorter ones; for, as I have said, many of these were thrown aside, and I never saw them till I had the misery of looking over his writings after the hand that traced them was dust; and some were in the hands of others, and I never saw them till now. The subjects of the poems are often to me an unerring guide; but on other occasions I can only guess, by finding them in the pages of the same manuscript book that contains poems with the date of whose composition I am fully conversant. In the present arrangement all his poetical translations will be placed together at the end.

The loss of his early papers prevents my being able to give any of the poetry of his boyhood. Of the few I give as "Early Poems", the greater part were published with "Alastor"; some of them were written previously, some at the same period. The poem beginning 'Oh, there are spirits in the air' was addressed in idea to Coleridge, whom he never knew; and at whose character he could only guess imperfectly, through his writings, and accounts he heard of him from some who knew him well. He regarded his change of opinions as rather an act of will than conviction, and believed that in his inner heart he would be haunted by what Shelley considered the better and holier aspirations of his youth. The summer evening that suggested to him the poem written in the churchyard of Lechlade occurred during his voyage up the Thames in 1815. He had been advised by a physician to live as much as possible in the open air; and a fortnight of a bright warm July was spent in tracing the Thames to its source. He never spent a season more tranquilly than the summer of 1815. He had just recovered from a severe pulmonary attack; the weather was warm and pleasant. He lived near Windsor Forest; and his life was spent under its shades or on the water, meditating subjects for verse. Hitherto, he had chiefly aimed at extending his political doctrines, and attempted so to do by appeals in prose essays to the people, exhorting them to claim their rights; but he had now begun to feel that the time for action was not ripe in England, and that the pen was the only instrument wherewith to prepare the way for better things.

In the scanty journals kept during those years I find a record of the books that Shelley read during several years. During the years of 1814 and 1815 the list is extensive. It includes, in Greek, Homer, Hesiod, Theocritus, the histories of Thucydides and Herodotus, and Diogenes Laertius. In Latin, Petronius, Suetonius, some of the works of Cicero, a large proportion of those of Seneca and Livy. In English, Milton's poems, Wordsworth's "Excursion", Southey's "Madoc" and "Thalaba", Locke "On the Human Understanding", Bacon's "Novum Organum". In Italian, Ariosto, Tasso, and Alfieri. In French, the "Reveries d'un Solitaire" of Rousseau. To these may be added several modern books of travel. He read few novels.

NOTE ON POEMS OF 1816, BY MRS. SHELLEY.

Shelley wrote little during this year. The poem entitled "The Sunset" was written in the spring of the year, while still residing at Bishopsgate. He spent the summer on the shores of the Lake of Geneva. The "Hymn to Intellectual Beauty" was conceived during his voyage round the lake with Lord Byron. He occupied himself during this voyage by reading the "Nouvelle Heloise" for the first time. The reading it on the very spot where the scenes are laid added to the interest; and he was at once surprised and charmed by the passionate eloquence and earnest enthralling interest that pervade this work. There was something in the character of Saint-Preux, in his abnegation of self, and in the worship he paid to Love, that coincided with Shelley's own disposition; and, though differing in many of the views and shocked by others, yet the effect of the whole was fascinating and delightful.

"Mont Blanc" was inspired by a view of that mountain and its surrounding peaks and valleys, as he lingered on the Bridge of Arve on his way through the Valley of Chamouni. Shelley makes the following mention of this poem in his publication of the "History of a Six Weeks' Tour, and Letters from Switzerland": 'The poem entitled "Mont Blanc" is written by the author of the two letters from Chamouni and Vevai. It was composed under the immediate impression of the deep and powerful feelings excited by the objects which it attempts to describe; and, as an undisciplined overflowing of the soul, rests its claim to approbation on an attempt to imitate the untamable wildness and inaccessible solemnity from which those feelings sprang.'

This was an eventful year, and less time was given to study than usual. In the list of his reading I find, in Greek, Theocritus, the "Prometheus" of Aeschylus, several of Plutarch's "Lives", and the works of Lucian. In Latin, Lucretius, Pliny's "Letters", the "Annals" and

"Germany" of Tacitus. In French, the "History of the French Revolution" by Lacretelle. He read for the first time, this year, Montaigne's "Essays", and regarded them ever after as one of the most delightful and instructive books in the world. The list is scanty in English works: Locke's "Essay", "Political Justice", and Coleridge's "Lay Sermon", form nearly the whole. It was his frequent habit to read aloud to me in the evening; in this way we read, this year, the New Testament, "Paradise Lost", Spenser's "Faery Queen", and "Don Quixote".

NOTE ON POEMS OF 1817, BY MRS. SHELLEY.

The very illness that oppressed, and the aspect of death which had approached so near Shelley, appear to have kindled to yet keener life the Spirit of Poetry in his heart. The restless thoughts kept awake by pain clothed themselves in verse. Much was composed during this year. The "Revolt of Islam", written and printed, was a great effort--"Rosalind and Helen" was begun--and the fragments and poems I can trace to the same period show how full of passion and reflection were his solitary hours.

In addition to such poems as have an intelligible aim and shape, many a stray idea and transitory emotion found imperfect and abrupt expression, and then again lost themselves in silence. As he never wandered without a book and without implements of writing, I find many such, in his manuscript books, that scarcely bear record; while some of them, broken and vague as they are, will appear valuable to those who love Shelley's mind, and desire to trace its workings.

He projected also translating the "Hymns" of Homer; his version of several of the shorter ones remains, as well as that to Mercury already published in the "Posthumous Poems". His readings this year were chiefly Greek. Besides the "Hymns" of Homer and the "Iliad", he read the dramas of Aeschylus and Sophocles, the "Symposium" of Plato, and Arrian's

"Historia Indica". In Latin, Apuleius alone is named. In English, the Bible was his constant study; he read a great portion of it aloud in the evening. Among these evening readings I find also mentioned the "Faerie Queen"; and other modern works, the production of his contemporaries, Coleridge, Wordsworth, Moore and Byron.

His life was now spent more in thought than action--he had lost the eager spirit which believed it could achieve what it projected for the benefit of mankind. And yet in the converse of daily life Shelley was far from being a melancholy man. He was eloquent when philosophy or politics or taste were the subjects of conversation. He was playful; and indulged in the wild spirit that mocked itself and others--not in bitterness, but in sport. The author of "Nightmare Abbey" seized on some points of his character and some habits of his life when he painted Scythrop. He was not addicted to 'port or madeira,' but in youth he had read of 'Illuminati and Eleutherarchs,' and believed that he possessed the power of operating an immediate change in the minds of men and the state of society. These wild dreams had faded; sorrow and adversity had struck home; but he struggled with despondency as he did with physical pain. There are few who remember him sailing paper boats, and watching the navigation of his tiny craft with eagerness--or repeating with wild energy "The Ancient Mariner", and Southey's "Old Woman of Berkeley"; but those who do will recollect that it was in such, and in the creations of his own fancy when that was most daring and ideal, that he sheltered himself from the storms and disappointments, the pain and sorrow, that beset his life.

No words can express the anguish he felt when his elder children were torn from him. In his first resentment against the Chancellor, on the passing of the decree, he had written a curse, in which there breathes, besides haughty indignation, all the tenderness of a father's love, which could imagine and fondly dwell upon its loss and the consequences.

At one time, while the question was still pending, the Chancellor had said some words that seemed to intimate that Shelley should not be permitted the care of any of his children, and for a moment he feared that our infant son would be torn from us. He did not hesitate to resolve, if such were menaced, to abandon country, fortune, everything, and to escape with his child; and I find some unfinished stanzas addressed to this son, whom afterwards we lost at Rome, written under the idea that we might suddenly be forced to cross the sea, so to preserve him. This poem, as well as the one previously quoted, were not written to exhibit the pangs of distress to the public; they were the spontaneous outbursts of a man who brooded over his wrongs and woes, and was impelled to shed the grace of his genius over the uncontrollable emotions of his heart. I ought to observe that the fourth verse of this effusion is introduced in "Rosalind and Helen". When afterwards this child died at Rome, he wrote, a propos of the English burying-ground in that city: 'This spot is the repository of a sacred loss, of which the yearnings of a parent's heart are now prophetic; he is rendered immortal by love, as his memory is by death. My beloved child lies buried here. I envy death the body far less than the oppressors the minds of those whom they have torn from me. The one can only kill the body, the other crushes the affections.'

NOTE ON POEMS OF 1818, BY MRS. SHELLEY.

We often hear of persons disappointed by a first visit to Italy. This was not Shelley's case. The aspect of its nature, its sunny sky, its majestic storms, of the luxuriant vegetation of the country, and the noble marble-built cities, enchanted him. The sight of the works of art was full enjoyment and wonder. He had not studied pictures or statues before; he now did so with the eye of taste, that referred not to the rules of schools, but to those of Nature and truth. The first entrance to Rome opened to him a scene of remains of antique grandeur that far surpassed his expectations; and the unspeakable beauty of Naples and its environs added to the impression he received of the transcendent and glorious beauty of Italy.

Our winter was spent at Naples. Here he wrote the fragments of "Marenghi" and "The Woodman and the Nightingale", which he afterwards threw aside. At this time, Shelley suffered greatly in health. He put himself under the care of a medical man, who promised great things, and made him endure severe bodily pain, without any good results. Constant and poignant physical suffering exhausted him; and though he preserved the appearance of cheerfulness, and often greatly enjoyed our wanderings in the environs of Naples, and our excursions on its sunny sea, yet many hours were passed when his thoughts, shadowed by illness, became gloomy,--and then he escaped to solitude, and in verses, which he hid from fear of wounding me, poured forth morbid but too natural bursts of discontent and sadness. One looks back with unspeakable regret and gnawing remorse to such periods; fancying that, had one been more alive to the nature of his feelings, and more attentive to soothe them, such would not have existed. And yet, enjoying as he appeared to do every sight or influence of earth or sky, it was difficult to imagine that any melancholy he showed was aught but the effect of the constant pain to which he was a martyr.

We lived in utter solitude. And such is often not the nurse of cheerfulness; for then, at least with those who have been exposed to adversity, the mind broods over its sorrows too intently; while the society of the enlightened, the witty, and the wise, enables us to forget ourselves by making us the sharers of the thoughts of others, which is a portion of the philosophy of happiness. Shelley never liked society in numbers,--it harassed and wearied him; but neither did he like loneliness, and usually, when alone, sheltered himself against memory and reflection in a book. But, with one or two whom he loved, he gave way to wild and joyous spirits, or in more serious conversation expounded his opinions with vivacity and eloquence. If an argument arose, no man ever argued better. He was clear, logical, and earnest, in supporting his own views; attentive, patient, and impartial, while listening to those on the adverse side. Had not a wall of prejudice been raised at this time between him and his countrymen, how many would have sought the acquaintance of one whom to know was to love and to revere! How many of the more enlightened of his contemporaries have since regretted that they did not seek him! how very few knew his worth while he lived! and, of those few, several were withheld by timidity or envy from declaring their sense of it. But no man was ever more enthusiastically loved--more looked up to, as one superior to his fellows in intellectual endowments and moral worth, by the few who knew him well, and had sufficient nobleness of soul to appreciate his superiority. His excellence is now acknowledged; but, even while admitted, not duly appreciated. For who, except those who were acquainted with him, can imagine his unwearied benevolence, his generosity, his systematic forbearance? And still less is his vast superiority in intellectual attainments sufficiently understood--his sagacity, his clear understanding, his learning, his prodigious memory. All these as displayed in conversation, were known to few while he lived, and are now silent in the tomb:

> 'Ahi orbo mondo ingrato!
> Gran cagion hai di dever pianger meco;
> Che quel ben ch' era in te, perdut' hai seco.'

NOTE ON POEMS OF 1819, BY MRS. SHELLEY.

Shelley loved the People; and respected them as often more virtuous, as always more suffering, and therefore more deserving of sympathy, than the great. He believed that a clash between the two classes of society was inevitable, and he eagerly ranged himself on the people's side. He had an idea of publishing a series of poems adapted expressly to commemorate their circumstances and wrongs. He wrote a few; but, in those days of prosecution for libel, they could not be printed. They are not among the best of his productions, a writer being always shackled when he endeavours to write down to the comprehension of those who could not understand or feel a highly imaginative style; but they show his earnestness, and with what heart-felt compassion he went home to the direct point of injury--that oppression is detestable as being the parent of starvation, nakedness, and ignorance. Besides these outpourings of compassion and indignation, he had meant to adorn the cause he loved with loftier poetry of glory and triumph: such is the scope of the "Ode to the Assertors of Liberty". He sketched also a new version of our national anthem, as addressed to Liberty.

NOTE ON POEMS OF 1820, BY MRS. SHELLEY.

We spent the latter part of the year 1819 in Florence, where Shelley passed several hours daily in the Gallery, and made various notes on its ancient works of art. His thoughts were a good deal taken up also by the project of a steamboat, undertaken by a friend, an engineer, to ply between Leghorn and Marseilles, for which he supplied a sum of money. This was a sort of plan to delight Shelley, and he was greatly disappointed when it was thrown aside.

There was something in Florence that disagreed excessively with his health, and he suffered far more pain than usual; so much so that we left it sooner than we intended, and removed to Pisa, where we had some friends, and, above all, where we could consult the celebrated Vacca as to the cause of Shelley's sufferings. He, like every other medical man, could only guess at that, and gave little hope of immediate relief; he enjoined him to abstain from all physicians and medicine, and to leave his complaint to Nature. As he had vainly consulted medical men of the highest repute in England, he was easily persuaded to adopt this advice. Pain and ill-health followed him to the end; but the residence at Pisa agreed with him better than any other, and there in consequence we remained.

In the Spring we spent a week or two near Leghorn, borrowing the house of some friends who were absent on a journey to England. It was on a beautiful summer evening, while wandering among the lanes whose myrtle-hedges were the bowers of the fire-flies, that we heard the carolling of the skylark which inspired one of the most beautiful of his poems. He addressed the letter to Mrs. Gisborne from this house, which was hers: he had made his study of the workshop of her son, who was an engineer. Mrs. Gisborne had been a friend of my father in her younger days. She was a lady of great accomplishments, and charming from her frank and affectionate nature. She had the most intense love of knowledge, a delicate and trembling sensibility, and preserved freshness of mind after a life of considerable adversity. As a favourite friend of my father, we had sought her with eagerness; and the most open and cordial friendship was established between us.

Our stay at the Baths of San Giuliano was shortened by an accident. At the foot of our garden ran the canal that communicated between the Serchio and the Arno. The Serchio overflowed its banks, and, breaking its bounds, this canal also overflowed; all this part of the country is below the level of its rivers, and the consequence was that it was speedily flooded. The rising waters filled the Square of the Baths, in the lower part of which our house was situated. The canal overflowed in the garden behind; the rising waters on either side at last burst open the doors, and, meeting in the house, rose to the height of six feet. It was a picturesque sight at night to see the peasants driving the cattle from the plains below to the hills above the Baths. A fire was kept up to guide them across the ford; and the forms of the men and the animals showed in dark relief against the red glare of the flame, which was reflected again in the waters that filled the Square.

We then removed to Pisa, and took up our abode there for the winter. The extreme mildness of the climate suited Shelley, and his solitude was enlivened by an intercourse with several intimate friends. Chance cast us strangely enough on this quiet half-unpeopled town; but its very peace suited Shelley. Its river, the near mountains, and not distant sea, added to its attractions, and were the objects of many delightful excursions. We feared the south of Italy, and a hotter climate, on account of our child; our former bereavement inspiring us with terror. We seemed to take root here, and moved little afterwards; often, indeed, entertaining projects for visiting other parts of Italy, but still delaying. But for our fears on account of our child, I believe we should have wandered over the world, both being passionately fond of travelling. But human life, besides its great unalterable necessities, is ruled by a thousand lilliputian ties that shackle at the time, although it is difficult to account afterwards for their influence over our destiny.

NOTE ON POEMS OF 1821, BY MRS. SHELLEY.

My task becomes inexpressibly painful as the year draws near that which sealed our earthly fate, and each poem, and each event it records, has a real or mysterious connection with the fatal catastrophe. I feel that I am incapable of putting on paper the history of those times. The heart of the man, abhorred of the poet, who could

'peep and botanize
Upon his mother's grave,'

does not appear to me more inexplicably framed than that of one who can dissect and probe past woes, and repeat to the public ear the groans drawn from them in the throes of their agony.

The year 1821 was spent in Pisa, or at the Baths of San Giuliano. We were not, as our wont had been, alone; friends had gathered round us.

Nearly all are dead, and, when Memory recurs to the past, she wanders among tombs. The genius, with all his blighting errors and mighty powers; the companion of Shelley's ocean-wanderings, and the sharer of his fate, than whom no man ever existed more gentle, generous, and fearless; and others, who found in Shelley's society, and in his great knowledge and warm sympathy, delight, instruction, and solace; have joined him beyond the grave. A few survive who have felt life a desert since he left it. What misfortune can equal death? Change can convert every other into a blessing, or heal its sting--death alone has no cure. It shakes the foundations of the earth on which we tread; it destroys its beauty; it casts down our shelter; it exposes us bare to desolation. When those we love have passed into eternity, 'life is the desert and the solitude' in which we are forced to linger--but never find comfort more.

There is much in the "Adonais" which seems now more applicable to Shelley himself than to the young and gifted poet whom he mourned. The poetic view he takes of death, and the lofty scorn he displays towards his calumniators, are as a prophecy on his own destiny when received among immortal names, and the poisonous breath of critics has vanished into emptiness before the fame he inherits.

Shelley's favourite taste was boating; when living near the Thames or by the Lake of Geneva, much of his life was spent on the water. On the shore of every lake or stream or sea near which he dwelt, he had a boat moored. He had latterly enjoyed this pleasure again. There are no pleasure-boats on the Arno; and the shallowness of its waters (except in winter-time, when the stream is too turbid and impetuous for boating) rendered it difficult to get any skiff light enough to float. Shelley, however, overcame the difficulty; he, together with a friend, contrived a boat such as the huntsmen carry about with them in the Maremma, to cross the sluggish but deep streams that intersect the forests,--a boat of laths and pitched canvas. It held three persons; and he was often seen on the Arno in it, to the horror of the Italians, who remonstrated on the danger, and could not understand how anyone could take pleasure in an exercise that risked life. 'Ma va per la vita!' they exclaimed. I little thought how true their words would prove. He once ventured, with a friend, on the glassy sea of a calm day, down the Arno and round the coast to Leghorn, which, by keeping close in shore, was very practicable. They returned to Pisa by the canal, when, missing the direct cut, they got entangled among weeds, and the boat upset; a wetting was all the harm done, except that the intense cold of his drenched clothes made Shelley faint. Once I went down with him to the mouth of the Arno, where the stream, then high and swift, met the tideless sea, and disturbed its sluggish waters. It was a waste and dreary scene; the desert sand stretched into a point surrounded by waves that broke idly though perpetually around; it was a scene very similar to Lido, of which he had said--

'I love all waste
And solitary places; where we taste
The pleasure of believing what we see
Is boundless, as we wish our souls to be:
And such was this wide ocean, and this shore
More barren than its billows.'

Our little boat was of greater use, unaccompanied by any danger, when we removed to the Baths. Some friends lived at the village of Pugnano, four miles off, and we went to and fro to see them, in our boat, by the canal; which, fed by the Serchio, was, though an artificial, a full and picturesque stream, making its way under verdant banks, sheltered by trees that dipped their boughs into the murmuring waters. By day, multitudes of Ephemera darted to and fro on the surface; at night, the fireflies came out among the shrubs on the banks; the cicale at noon-day kept up their hum; the aziola cooed in the quiet evening. It was a pleasant summer, bright in all but Shelley's health and inconstant spirits; yet he enjoyed himself greatly, and became more and more attached to the part of the country were chance appeared to cast us. Sometimes he projected taking a farm situated on the height of one of the near hills, surrounded by chestnut and pine woods, and overlooking a wide extent of country: or settling still farther in the maritime Apennines, at Massa. Several of his slighter and unfinished poems were inspired by these scenes, and by the companions around us. It is the nature of that poetry, however, which overflows from the soul oftener to express sorrow and regret than joy; for it is when oppressed by the weight of life, and away from those he loves, that the poet has recourse to the solace of expression in verse.

Still, Shelley's passion was the ocean; and he wished that our summers, instead of being passed among the hills near Pisa, should be spent on the shores of the sea. It was very difficult to find a spot. We shrank from Naples from a fear that the heats would disagree with Percy: Leghorn had lost its only attraction, since our friends who had resided there were returned to England; and, Monte Nero being the resort of many English, we did not wish to find ourselves in the midst of a colony of chance travellers. No one then thought it possible to reside at Via Reggio, which latterly has become a summer resort. The low lands and bad air of Maremma stretch the whole length of the western shores of the Mediterranean, till broken by the rocks and hills of Spezia. It was a vague idea, but Shelley suggested an excursion to Spezia, to see whether it would be feasible to spend a summer there. The beauty of the bay enchanted him. We saw no house to suit us; but the notion took root, and many circumstances, enchained as by fatality, occurred to urge him to execute it.

He looked forward this autumn with great pleasure to the prospect of a visit from Leigh Hunt. When Shelley visited Lord Byron at Ravenna, the latter had suggested his coming out, together with the plan of a periodical work in which they should all join. Shelley saw a prospect of good for the fortunes of his friend, and pleasure in his society; and instantly exerted himself to have the plan executed. He did not intend himself joining in the work: partly from pride, not wishing to have the air of acquiring readers for his poetry by associating it with the compositions of more popular writers; and also because he might feel shackled in the free expression of his opinions, if any friends were to be compromised. By those opinions, carried even to their outermost extent, he wished to live and die, as being in his conviction not only true, but such as alone would conduce to the moral improvement and happiness of mankind. The sale of the work might meanwhile, either really or supposedly, be injured by the free expression of his thoughts; and this evil he resolved to avoid.

NOTE ON POEMS OF 1822, BY MRS. SHELLEY.

This morn thy gallant bark
Sailed on a sunny sea:
'Tis noon, and tempests dark
Have wrecked it on the lee.
Ah woe! ah woe!
By Spirits of the deep
Thou'rt cradled on the billow
To thy eternal sleep.

Thou sleep'st upon the shore
Beside the knelling surge,
And Sea-nymphs evermore
Shall sadly chant thy dirge.
They come, they come,
The Spirits of the deep,--
While near thy seaweed pillow
My lonely watch I keep.

From far across the sea
I hear a loud lament,
By Echo's voice for thee
From Ocean's caverns sent.
O list! O list!
The Spirits of the deep!
They raise a wail of sorrow,
While I forever weep.

With this last year of the life of Shelley these Notes end. They are not
what I intended them to be. I began with energy, and a burning desire to
impart to the world, in worthy language, the sense I have of the virtues
and genius of the beloved and the lost; my strength has failed under the
task. Recurrence to the past, full of its own deep and unforgotten joys
and sorrows, contrasted with succeeding years of painful and solitary
struggle, has shaken my health. Days of great suffering have followed my
attempts to write, and these again produced a weakness and languor that
spread their sinister influence over these notes. I dislike speaking of
myself, but cannot help apologizing to the dead, and to the public, for
not having executed in the manner I desired the history I engaged to
give of Shelley's writings. (I at one time feared that the correction of
the press might be less exact through my illness; but I believe that it
is nearly free from error. Some asterisks occur in a few pages, as they
did in the volume of "Posthumous Poems", either because they refer to
private concerns, or because the original manuscript was left imperfect.
Did any one see the papers from which I drew that volume, the wonder
would be how any eyes or patience were capable of extracting it from so
confused a mass, interlined and broken into fragments, so that the sense
could only be deciphered and joined by guesses which might seem rather
intuitive than founded on reasoning. Yet I believe no mistake was made.)

The winter of 1822 was passed in Pisa, if we might call that season
winter in which autumn merged into spring after the interval of but few

days of bleaker weather. Spring sprang up early, and with extreme beauty. Shelley had conceived the idea of writing a tragedy on the subject of Charles I. It was one that he believed adapted for a drama; full of intense interest, contrasted character, and busy passion. He had recommended it long before, when he encouraged me to attempt a play. Whether the subject proved more difficult than he anticipated, or whether in fact he could not bend his mind away from the broodings and wanderings of thought, divested from human interest, which he best loved, I cannot tell; but he proceeded slowly, and threw it aside for one of the most mystical of his poems, the "Triumph of Life", on which he was employed at the last.

His passion for boating was fostered at this time by having among our friends several sailors. His favourite companion, Edward Ellerker Williams, of the 8th Light Dragoons, had begun his life in the navy, and had afterwards entered the army; he had spent several years in India, and his love for adventure and manly exercises accorded with Shelley's taste. It was their favourite plan to build a boat such as they could manage themselves, and, living on the sea-coast, to enjoy at every hour and season the pleasure they loved best. Captain Roberts, R.N., undertook to build the boat at Genoa, where he was also occupied in building the "Bolivar" for Lord Byron. Ours was to be an open boat, on a model taken from one of the royal dockyards. I have since heard that there was a defect in this model, and that it was never seaworthy. In the month of February, Shelley and his friend went to Spezia to seek for houses for us. Only one was to be found at all suitable; however, a trifle such as not finding a house could not stop Shelley; the one found was to serve for all. It was unfurnished; we sent our furniture by sea, and with a good deal of precipitation, arising from his impatience, made our removal. We left Pisa on the 26th of April.

The Bay of Spezia is of considerable extent, and divided by a rocky promontory into a larger and smaller one. The town of Lerici is situated on the eastern point, and in the depth of the smaller bay, which bears the name of this town, is the village of San Terenzo. Our house, Casa Magni, was close to this village; the sea came up to the door, a steep hill sheltered it behind. The proprietor of the estate on which it was situated was insane; he had begun to erect a large house at the summit of the hill behind, but his malady prevented its being finished, and it was falling into ruin. He had (and this to the Italians had seemed a glaring symptom of very decided madness) rooted up the olives on the hillside, and planted forest trees. These were mostly young, but the plantation was more in English taste than I ever elsewhere saw in Italy; some fine walnut and ilex trees intermingled their dark massy foliage, and formed groups which still haunt my memory, as then they satiated the eye with a sense of loveliness. The scene was indeed of unimaginable beauty. The blue extent of waters, the almost landlocked bay, the near castle of Lerici shutting it in to the east, and distant Porto Venere to the west; the varied forms of the precipitous rocks that bound in the beach, over which there was only a winding rugged footpath towards Lerici, and none on the other side; the tideless sea leaving no sands nor shingle, formed a picture such as one sees in Salvator Rosa's landscapes only. Sometimes the sunshine vanished when the sirocco raged--the 'ponente' the wind was called on that shore. The gales and squalls that hailed our first arrival surrounded the bay with foam; the howling wind swept round our exposed house, and the sea roared unremittingly, so that we almost fancied ourselves on board ship. At other times sunshine and calm invested sea and sky, and the rich tints of Italian heaven bathed the scene in bright and ever-varying tints.

The natives were wilder than the place. Our near neighbours of San Terenzo were more like savages than any people I ever before lived among. Many a night they passed on the beach, singing, or rather howling; the women dancing about among the waves that broke at their feet, the men leaning against the rocks and joining in their loud wild chorus. We could get no provisions nearer than Sarzana, at a distance of three miles and a half off, with the torrent of the Magra between; and even there the supply was very deficient. Had we been wrecked on an island of the South Seas, we could scarcely have felt ourselves farther from civilisation and comfort; but, where the sun shines, the latter becomes an unnecessary luxury, and we had enough society among ourselves. Yet I confess housekeeping became rather a toilsome task, especially as I was suffering in my health, and could not exert myself actively.

At first the fatal boat had not arrived, and was expected with great impatience. On Monday, 12th May, it came. Williams records the long-wished-for fact in his journal: 'Cloudy and threatening weather. M. Maglian called; and after dinner, and while walking with him on the terrace, we discovered a strange sail coming round the point of Porto Venere, which proved at length to be Shelley's boat. She had left Genoa on Thursday last, but had been driven back by the prevailing bad winds. A Mr. Heslop and two English seamen brought her round, and they speak most highly of her performances. She does indeed excite my surprise and admiration. Shelley and I walked to Lerici, and made a stretch off the land to try her: and I find she fetches whatever she looks at. In short, we have now a perfect plaything for the summer.'--It was thus that short-sighted mortals welcomed Death, he having disguised his grim form in a pleasing mask! The time of the friends was now spent on the sea; the weather became fine, and our whole party often passed the evenings on the water when the wind promised pleasant sailing. Shelley and Williams made longer excursions; they sailed several times to Massa. They had engaged one of the seamen who brought her round, a boy, by name Charles Vivian; and they had not the slightest apprehension of danger. When the weather was unfavourable, they employed themselves with alterations in the rigging, and by building a boat of canvas and reeds, as light as possible, to have on board the other for the convenience of landing in waters too shallow for the larger vessel. When Shelley was on board, he had his papers with him; and much of the "Triumph of Life" was written as he sailed or weltered on that sea which was soon to engulf him.

The heats set in in the middle of June; the days became excessively hot. But the sea-breeze cooled the air at noon, and extreme heat always put Shelley in spirits. A long drought had preceded the heat; and prayers for rain were being put up in the churches, and processions of relics for the same effect took place in every town. At this time we received letters announcing the arrival of Leigh Hunt at Genoa. Shelley was very eager to see him. I was confined to my room by severe illness, and could not move; it was agreed that Shelley and Williams should go to Leghorn in the boat. Strange that no fear of danger crossed our minds! Living on the sea-shore, the ocean became as a plaything: as a child may sport with a lighted stick, till a spark inflames a forest, and spreads destruction over all, so did we fearlessly and blindly tamper with danger, and make a game of the terrors of the ocean. Our Italian neighbours, even, trusted themselves as far as Massa in the skiff; and the running down the line of coast to Leghorn gave no more notion of peril than a fair-weather inland navigation would have done to those who had never seen the sea. Once, some months before, Trelawny had raised a warning voice as to the difference of our calm bay and the open sea beyond; but Shelley and his friend, with their one sailor-boy, thought themselves a match for the storms of the Mediterranean, in a boat which they looked upon as equal to all it was put to do.

On the 1st of July they left us. If ever shadow of future ill darkened the present hour, such was over my mind when they went. During the whole of our stay at Lerici, an intense presentiment of coming evil brooded over my mind, and covered this beautiful place and genial summer with the shadow of coming misery. I had vainly struggled with these emotions--they seemed accounted for by my illness; but at this hour of separation they recurred with renewed violence. I did not anticipate danger for them, but a vague expectation of evil shook me to agony, and

I could scarcely bring myself to let them go. The day was calm and clear; and, a fine breeze rising at twelve, they weighed for Leghorn. They made the run of about fifty miles in seven hours and a half. The "Bolivar" was in port; and, the regulations of the Health-office not permitting them to go on shore after sunset, they borrowed cushions from the larger vessel, and slept on board their boat.

They spent a week at Pisa and Leghorn. The want of rain was severely felt in the country. The weather continued sultry and fine. I have heard that Shelley all this time was in brilliant spirits. Not long before, talking of presentiment, he had said the only one that he ever found infallible was the certain advent of some evil fortune when he felt peculiarly joyous. Yet, if ever fate whispered of coming disaster, such inaudible but not unfelt prognostics hovered around us. The beauty of the place seemed unearthly in its excess: the distance we were at from all signs of civilization, the sea at our feet, its murmurs or its roaring for ever in our ears,--all these things led the mind to brood over strange thoughts, and, lifting it from everyday life, caused it to be familiar with the unreal. A sort of spell surrounded us; and each day, as the voyagers did not return, we grew restless and disquieted, and yet, strange to say, we were not fearful of the most apparent danger.

The spell snapped; it was all over; an interval of agonizing doubt--of days passed in miserable journeys to gain tidings, of hopes that took firmer root even as they were more baseless--was changed to the certainty of the death that eclipsed all happiness for the survivors for evermore.

There was something in our fate peculiarly harrowing. The remains of those we lost were cast on shore; but, by the quarantine-laws of the coast, we were not permitted to have possession of them--the law with respect to everything cast on land by the sea being that such should be burned, to prevent the possibility of any remnant bringing the plague into Italy; and no representation could alter the law. At length, through the kind and unwearied exertions of Mr. Dawkins, our Charge d'Affaires at Florence, we gained permission to receive the ashes after the bodies were consumed. Nothing could equal the zeal of Trelawny in carrying our wishes into effect. He was indefatigable in his exertions, and full of forethought and sagacity in his arrangements. It was a fearful task; he stood before us at last, his hands scorched and blistered by the flames of the funeral-pyre, and by touching the burnt relics as he placed them in the receptacles prepared for the purpose. And there, in compass of that small case, was gathered all that remained on earth of him whose genius and virtue were a crown of glory to the world--whose love had been the source of happiness, peace, and good,--to be buried with him!

The concluding stanzas of the "Adonais" pointed out where the remains ought to be deposited; in addition to which our beloved child lay buried in the cemetery at Rome. Thither Shelley's ashes were conveyed; and they rest beneath one of the antique weed-grown towers that recur at intervals in the circuit of the massy ancient wall of Rome. He selected the hallowed place himself; there is

> 'the sepulchre,
> Oh, not of him, but of our joy!--
> ...
> And gray walls moulder round, on which dull Time
> Feeds, like slow fire upon a hoary brand;
> And one keen pyramid with wedge sublime,
> Pavilioning the dust of him who planned
> This refuge for his memory, doth stand
> Like flame transformed to marble; and beneath,
> A field is spread, on which a newer band
> Have pitched in Heaven's smile their camp of death,

Welcoming him we lose with scarce extinguished breath.'

Could sorrow for the lost, and shuddering anguish at the vacancy left behind, be soothed by poetic imaginations, there was something in Shelley's fate to mitigate pangs which yet, alas! could not be so mitigated; for hard reality brings too miserably home to the mourner all that is lost of happiness, all of lonely unsolaced struggle that remains. Still, though dreams and hues of poetry cannot blunt grief, it invests his fate with a sublime fitness, which those less nearly allied may regard with complacency. A year before he had poured into verse all such ideas about death as give it a glory of its own. He had, as it now seems, almost anticipated his own destiny; and, when the mind figures his skiff wrapped from sight by the thunder-storm, as it was last seen upon the purple sea, and then, as the cloud of the tempest passed away, no sign remained of where it had been (Captain Roberts watched the vessel with his glass from the top of the lighthouse of Leghorn, on its homeward track. They were off Via Reggio, at some distance from shore, when a storm was driven over the sea. It enveloped them and several larger vessels in darkness. When the cloud passed onwards, Roberts looked again, and saw every other vessel sailing on the ocean except their little schooner, which had vanished. From that time he could scarcely doubt the fatal truth; yet we fancied that they might have been driven towards Elba or Corsica, and so be saved. The observation made as to the spot where the boat disappeared caused it to be found, through the exertions of Trelawny for that effect. It had gone down in ten fathom water; it had not capsized, and, except such things as had floated from her, everything was found on board exactly as it had been placed when they sailed. The boat itself was uninjured. Roberts possessed himself of her, and decked her; but she proved not seaworthy, and her shattered planks now lie rotting on the shore of one of the Ionian islands, on which she was wrecked.)--who but will regard as a prophecy the last stanza of the "Adonais"?

'The breath whose might I have invoked in song
Descends on me; my spirit's bark is driven,
Far from the shore, far from the trembling throng
Whose sails were never to the tempest given;
The massy earth and sphered skies are riven!
I am borne darkly, fearfully, afar;
Whilst burning through the inmost veil of Heaven,
The soul of Adonais, like a star,
Beacons from the abode where the Eternal are.'

Putney, May 1, 1839.

The Codes Of Hammurabi And Moses
W. W. Davies

QTY

The discovery of the Hammurabi Code is one of the greatest achievements of archaeology, and is of paramount interest, not only to the student of the Bible, but also to all those interested in ancient history...

Religion　　ISBN: *1-59462-338-4*　　**Pages:132**

MSRP $12.95

The Theory of Moral Sentiments
Adam Smith

QTY

This work from 1749. contains original theories of conscience amd moral judgment and it is the foundation for systemof morals.

Philosophy　ISBN: *1-59462-777-0*　　**Pages:536**

MSRP $19.95

Jessica's First Prayer
Hesba Stretton

QTY

In a screened and secluded corner of one of the many railway-bridges which span the streets of London there could be seen a few years ago, from five o'clock every morning until half past eight, a tidily set-out coffee-stall, consisting of a trestle and board, upon which stood two large tin cans, with a small fire of charcoal burning under each so as to keep the coffee boiling during the early hours of the morning when the work-people were thronging into the city on their way to their daily toil...

Pages:84

Childrens　ISBN: *1-59462-373-2*　*MSRP $9.95*

My Life and Work
Henry Ford

QTY

Henry Ford revolutionized the world with his implementation of mass production for the Model T automobile. Gain valuable business insight into his life and work with his own auto-biography... "We have only started on our development of our country we have not as yet, with all our talk of wonderful progress, done more than scratch the surface. The progress has been wonderful enough but..."

Pages:300

Biographies/　ISBN: *1-59462-198-5*　*MSRP $21.95*

The Art of Cross-Examination
Francis Wellman

QTY

I presume it is the experience of every author, after his first book is published upon an important subject, to be almost overwhelmed with a wealth of ideas and illustrations which could readily have been included in his book, and which to his own mind, at least, seem to make a second edition inevitable. Such certainly was the case with me; and when the first edition had reached its sixth impression in five months, I rejoiced to learn that it seemed to my publishers that the book had met with a sufficiently favorable reception to justify a second and considerably enlarged edition. ..

Pages:412

Reference **ISBN: *1-59462-647-2*** *MSRP $19.95*

On the Duty of Civil Disobedience
Henry David Thoreau

QTY

Thoreau wrote his famous essay, On the Duty of Civil Disobedience, as a protest against an unjust but popular war and the immoral but popular institution of slave-owning. He did more than write—he declined to pay his taxes, and was hauled off to gaol in consequence. Who can say how much this refusal of his hastened the end of the war and of slavery ?

Law **ISBN: *1-59462-747-9*** **Pages:48**

MSRP $7.45

Dream Psychology
Psychoanalysis for Beginners

Sigmund Freud

Dream Psychology Psychoanalysis for Beginners
Sigmund Freud

QTY

Sigmund Freud, born Sigismund Schlomo Freud (May 6, 1856 - September 23, 1939), was a Jewish-Austrian neurologist and psychiatrist who co-founded the psychoanalytic school of psychology. Freud is best known for his theories of the unconscious mind, especially involving the mechanism of repression; his redefinition of sexual desire as mobile and directed towards a wide variety of objects; and his therapeutic techniques, especially his understanding of transference in the therapeutic relationship and the presumed value of dreams as sources of insight into unconscious desires.

Pages:196

Psychology **ISBN: *1-59462-905-6*** *MSRP $15.45*

The Miracle of Right Thought
Orison Swett Marden

QTY

Believe with all of your heart that you will do what you were made to do. When the mind has once formed the habit of holding cheerful, happy, prosperous pictures, it will not be easy to form the opposite habit. It does not matter how improbable or how far away this realization may see, or how dark the prospects may be, if we visualize them as best we can, as vividly as possible, hold tenaciously to them and vigorously struggle to attain them, they will gradually become actualized, realized in the life. But a desire, a longing without endeavor, a yearning abandoned or held indifferently will vanish without realization.

Pages:360

Self Help **ISBN: *1-59462-644-8*** *MSRP $25.45*

The Rosicrucian Cosmo-Conception Mystic Christianity *by Max Heindel*   ISBN: *1-59462-188-8*   **$38.95**
The Rosicrucian Cosmo-conception is not dogmatic, neither does it appeal to any other authority than the reason of the student. It is: not controversial, but is: sent forth in the, hope that it may help to clear...   New Age/Religion Pages 646

Abandonment To Divine Providence *by Jean-Pierre de Caussade*   ISBN: *1-59462-228-0*   **$25.95**
"The Rev. Jean Pierre de Caussade was one of the most remarkable spiritual writers of the Society of Jesus in France in the 18th Century. His death took place at Toulouse in 1751. His works have gone through many editions and have been republished...   Inspirational/Religion Pages 400

Mental Chemistry *by Charles Haanel*   ISBN: *1-59462-192-6*   **$23.95**
Mental Chemistry allows the change of material conditions by combining and appropriately utilizing the power of the mind. Much like applied chemistry creates something new and unique out of careful combinations of chemicals the mastery of mental chemistry...   New Age Pages 354

The Letters of Robert Browning and Elizabeth Barret Barrett 1845-1846 vol II   ISBN: *1-59462-193-4*   **$35.95**
by Robert Browning and Elizabeth Barrett   Biographies Pages 596

Gleanings In Genesis (volume I) *by Arthur W. Pink*   ISBN: *1-59462-130-6*   **$27.45**
Appropriately has Genesis been termed "the seed plot of the Bible" for in it we have, in germ form, almost all of the great doctrines which are afterwards fully developed in the books of Scripture which follow...   Religion/Inspirational Pages 420

The Master Key *by L. W. de Laurence*   ISBN: *1-59462-001-6*   **$30.95**
In no branch of human knowledge has there been a more lively increase of the spirit of research during the past few years than in the study of Psychology, Concentration and Mental Discipline. The requests for authentic lessons in Thought Control, Mental Discipline and...   New Age/Business Pages 422

The Lesser Key Of Solomon Goetia *by L. W. de Laurence*   ISBN: *1-59462-092-X*   **$9.95**
This translation of the first book of the "Lernegton" which is now for the first time made accessible to students of Talismanic Magic was done, after careful collation and edition, from numerous Ancient Manuscripts in Hebrew, Latin, and French...   New Age/Occult Pages 92

Rubaiyat Of Omar Khayyam *by Edward Fitzgerald*   ISBN:*1-59462-332-5*   **$13.95**
Edward Fitzgerald, whom the world has already learned, in spite of his own efforts to remain within the shadow of anonymity, to look upon as one of the rarest poets of the century, was born at Bredfield, in Suffolk, on the 31st of March, 1809. He was the third son of John Purcell...   Music Pages 172

Ancient Law *by Henry Maine*   ISBN: *1-59462-128-4*   **$29.95**
The chief object of the following pages is to indicate some of the earliest ideas of mankind, as they are reflected in Ancient Law, and to point out the relation of those ideas to modern thought.   Religion/History Pages 452

Far-Away Stories *by William J. Locke*   ISBN: *1-59462-129-2*   **$19.45**
"Good wine needs no bush, but a collection of mixed vintages does. And this book is just such a collection. Some of the stories I do not want to remain buried for ever in the museum files of dead magazine-numbers an author's not unpardonable vanity..."   Fiction Pages 272

Life of David Crockett *by David Crockett*   ISBN: *1-59462-250-7*   **$27.45**
"Colonel David Crockett was one of the most remarkable men of the times in which he lived. Born in humble life, but gifted with a strong will, an indomitable courage, and unremitting perseverance...   Biographies/New Age Pages 424

Lip-Reading *by Edward Nitchie*   ISBN: *1-59462-206-X*   **$25.95**
Edward B. Nitchie, founder of the New York School for the Hard of Hearing, now the Nitchie School of Lip-Reading, Inc, wrote "LIP-READING Principles and Practice". The development and perfecting of this meritorious work on lip-reading was an undertaking...   How-to Pages 400

A Handbook of Suggestive Therapeutics, Applied Hypnotism, Psychic Science   ISBN: *1-59462-214-0*   **$24.95**
by Henry Munro   Health/New Age/Health/Self-help Pages 376

A Doll's House: and Two Other Plays *by Henrik Ibsen*   ISBN: *1-59462-112-8*   **$19.95**
Henrik Ibsen created this classic when in revolutionary 1848 Rome. Introducing some striking concepts in playwriting for the realist genre, this play has been studied the world over.   Fiction/Classics/Plays 308

The Light of Asia *by sir Edwin Arnold*   ISBN: *1-59462-204-3*   **$13.95**
In this poetic masterpiece, Edwin Arnold describes the life and teachings of Buddha. The man who was to become known as Buddha to the world was born as Prince Gautama of India but he rejected the worldly riches and abandoned the reigns of power when...   Religion/History/Biographies Pages 170

The Complete Works of Guy de Maupassant *by Guy de Maupassant*   ISBN: *1-59462-157-8*   **$16.95**
"For days and days, nights and nights, I had dreamed of that first kiss which was to consecrate our engagement, and I knew not on what spot I should put my lips..."   Fiction/Classics Pages 240

The Art of Cross-Examination *by Francis L. Wellman*   ISBN: *1-59462-309-0*   **$26.95**
Written by a renowned trial lawyer, Wellman imparts his experience and uses case studies to explain how to use psychology to extract desired information through questioning.   How-to/Science/Reference Pages 408

Answered or Unanswered? *by Louisa Vaughan*   ISBN: *1-59462-248-5*   **$10.95**
Miracles of Faith in China   Religion Pages 112

The Edinburgh Lectures on Mental Science (1909) *by Thomas*   ISBN: *1-59462-008-3*   **$11.95**
This book contains the substance of a course of lectures recently given by the writer in the Queen Street Hail, Edinburgh. Its purpose is to indicate the Natural Principles governing the relation between Mental Action and Material Conditions...   New Age/Psychology Pages 148

Ayesha *by H. Rider Haggard*   ISBN: *1-59462-301-5*   **$24.95**
Verily and indeed it is the unexpected that happens! Probably if there was one person upon the earth from whom the Editor of this, and of a certain previous history, did not expect to hear again...   Classics Pages 380

Ayala's Angel *by Anthony Trollope*   ISBN: *1-59462-352-X*   **$29.95**
The two girls were both pretty, but Lucy who was twenty-one who supposed to be simple and comparatively unattractive, whereas Ayala was credited, as her Bombwhat romantic name might show, with poetic charm and a taste for romance. Ayala when her father died was nineteen...   Fiction Pages 484

The American Commonwealth *by James Bryce*   ISBN: *1-59462-286-8*   **$34.45**
An interpretation of American democratic political theory. It examines political mechanics and society from the perspective of Scotsman James Bryce   Politics Pages 572

Stories of the Pilgrims *by Margaret P. Pumphrey*   ISBN: *1-59462-116-0*   **$17.95**
This book explores pilgrims religious oppression in England as well as their escape to Holland and eventual crossing to America on the Mayflower, and their early days in New England...   History Pages 268

QTY

The Fasting Cure *by Sinclair Upton*　　　　　　　　　　　ISBN: *1-59462-222-1*　**$13.95**
*In the Cosmopolitan Magazine for May, 1910, and in the Contemporary Review (London) for April, 1910, I published an article dealing with my experi-
ences in fasting. I have written a great many magazine articles, but never one which attracted so much attention...* New Age/Self Help/Health Pages 164

Hebrew Astrology *by Sepharial*　　　　　　　　　　　　ISBN: *1-59462-308-2*　**$13.45**
*In these days of advanced thinking it is a matter of common observation that we have left many of the old landmarks behind and that we are now pressing
forward to greater heights and to a wider horizon than that which represented the mind-content of our progenitors...* Astrology Pages 144

Thought Vibration or The Law of Attraction in the Thought World　ISBN: *1-59462-127-6*　**$12.95**

by William Walker Atkinson　　　　　　　　　　　　　　Psychology/Religion Pages 144

Optimism *by Helen Keller*　　　　　　　　　　　　　　ISBN: *1-59462-108-X*　**$15.95**
*Helen Keller was blind, deaf, and mute since 19 months old, yet famously learned how to overcome these handicaps, communicate with the world, and
spread her lectures promoting optimism. An inspiring read for everyone...* Biographies/Inspirational Pages 84

Sara Crewe *by Frances Burnett*　　　　　　　　　　　ISBN: *1-59462-360-0*　**$9.45**
*In the first place, Miss Minchin lived in London. Her home was a large, dull, tall one, in a large, dull square, where all the houses were alike, and all the
sparrows were alike, and where all the door-knockers made the same heavy sound...* Childrens/Classic Pages 88

The Autobiography of Benjamin Franklin *by Benjamin Franklin*　ISBN: *1-59462-135-7*　**$24.95**
*The Autobiography of Benjamin Franklin has probably been more extensively read than any other American historical work, and no other book of its kind
has had such ups and downs of fortune. Franklin lived for many years in England, where he was agent...* Biographies/History Pages 332

Name	
Email	
Telephone	
Address	
City, State ZIP	

☐ **Credit Card**　　　　☐ **Check / Money Order**

Credit Card Number	
Expiration Date	
Signature	

*Please Mail to:　Book Jungle
　　　　　　　　　PO Box 2226
　　　　　　　　　Champaign, IL 61825
　or Fax to:　　　630-214-0564*

ORDERING INFORMATION

web: *www.bookjungle.com*
email: *sales@bookjungle.com*
fax: *630-214-0564*
mail: *Book Jungle PO Box 2226 Champaign, IL 61825*
or PayPal *to sales@bookjungle.com*

Please contact us for bulk discounts

DIRECT-ORDER TERMS

**20% Discount if You Order
Two or More Books**
Free Domestic Shipping!
Accepted: Master Card, Visa,
Discover, American Express